THE MAN IN THE MIRROR

GEORGIA LE CARRE

ACKNOWLEDGMENTS

Many, many thanks for all your hard work,
Caryl Milton
Elizabeth Burns
Nichola Rhead
Teresa Banschbach
Hafsa Islam
Tracy Gray
Brittany Urbaniak

The Man In The Mirror

ISBN 978-1-910575-85-7

Blackmailed By The Beast
Submitting To The Billionaire
The Bad Boy Wants Me
Nanny & The Beast
His Frozen Heart

CHAPTER 1

CHARLOTTE

https://www.youtube.com/watch?v=f4Mc-NYPHaQ
I Want To Break Free

"I'm just sick of it now, April. I mean, this is like the sixth … no, hang on one minute, the *seventh* time, if I count that back-stabbing witch in Hammersmith, that I've been fired because the wife thinks something is going on between me and her fat, ugly husband."

April looked unsympathetic. "Listen, you can't have your cake and eat it too."

"What the hell is that supposed to mean?" I demanded.

"Look at you. Natural blonde hair, blue-eyes, a body to die for. Are you surprised that men keep falling for you and their wives hate you for it?"

I looked at her incredulously. "I can't even believe you said that. First of all, I don't have a body to die for. I have fat

1

thighs, and secondly, even if what you say is true, what would you have me do? Put on two hundred pounds and scratch my face to shreds so I can keep my job?"

She grinned. "You don't have fat thighs, you have adorably curvy thighs so stop being such a drama queen. How about we just dress you down for your next job?"

"Dress me down?" I huffed, hands on hips. "Have you not seen the shapeless sacks I wear to work?"

She gazed back unfazed. "Yes, I have, but the problem is the sackcloth just emphasizes your big, blue come-fuck-me eyes."

I rolled my eyes. "Right. I'll just gouge them out then, shall I?"

"Don't be so silly. How about glasses?" She reached for the tub of Pringles and opened it.

I took the Pringle she held out in her hand for me. "Glasses? I'd feel like a fool wearing glasses when I don't need them. But more importantly why should *I* do all this just because stupid men can't control themselves?"

"I thought you really wanted this job," April said.

I closed my come-fuck-me eyes. "Yes, I do. I really do. I loved Wales when I went there two years ago. No smog, no traffic noises. Hell, the air was so clean I didn't even have to clean my nose."

April laughed. "Why are you so strange, Charlotte?"

I looked into the distance dreamily. "Oh, and the people. They were all so friendly, big hearted, and happy. They were not sour-faced and rushing around in a mad dash the whole time. Heck, come to think of it, even the sheep had better personalities than some Londoners. And I absolutely loved the idea of walking for miles and miles without meeting a single person. It broke my heart when the family moved to America so I'd really, really love to go back and live in a castle in Wales again."

"Well, you got your wish."

I chewed my lower lip reflectively. "Yes, I did. I couldn't believe my luck when Christine called and told me about the job."

"Okay, but what was the other thing Christine told you?"

I sighed. "The mistress of the house could be a bit difficult. That she's some ex-beauty queen."

"A bit difficult? Ex-beauty queen? We both know what that means. If you really want to go back to Wales—"

"I do," I interrupted.

"Glasses it is. You know how it works. You're going into a woman's home and if you can quickly make her feel you are not a threat to her, she'll relax and let you get on with the job."

I nodded.

"But you never know, you might get there and find another completely lovely, secure wife like the one you went to before. Then you can ditch your glasses and sackcloth and just have fun with the kid."

"Okay," I agreed reluctantly. I really hated the idea that I had to pretend to be half-blind just so some insecure, jealous woman could feel good about hiring me and trusting me around her husband. I would *never ever* steal someone else's husband. That would just go against everything I believed in.

My mother brought me up right. But if I did have a husband I would never try to protect him from other women because in my books if he was so weak and uncommitted to me that he couldn't resist another woman's flesh then I was well rid of him.

"When are you going?" April interrupted my thoughts.

"I'm leaving on Monday."

"I'll miss you, you know?"

I laughed. "No, you won't. You haven't closed your legs since you met that Russian husband of yours. You won't even notice I'm gone."

"That's not even funny. Of course, I will miss you. Anyway, I don't even know why you insist on working so hard and still paying rent here. Yuri has already offered to buy you a fabulous house near us."

I smiled at her. April would never know how much I really love her. She is the sister I never had. "I know, but I like working. It makes me feel useful. I can't imagine being one of those women who has lunches and manicures instead of a job."

"Sure, I get that, but why won't you let Yuri buy an apartment for you instead of paying rent."

I shook my head resolutely. "Yuri made all my dreams come true when he bought my mom's house for her. I'll be forever grateful for that. I don't want anything else from him. The most important thing is he makes you happy."

She grinned. "That he does." She stopped suddenly, her eyes

widening. "Oh my God, the baby just moved again. I've got to tell Yuri this." She reached for her cell phone.

I groaned. "Oh, for god's sake, where is the vomit bucket? Do I have to listen to the two of you cooing at each other over the phone *again?*"

She pressed a button on her phone and looked at me smugly. "You better be careful young lady. I won't forget this when you find your man and go ga ga over him."

I snorted. "Hardly likely since I'll be dressed in a sackcloth, ashes, and a horrible pair of librarian glasses for the foreseeable future."

CHAPTER 2

BRETT

https://www.youtube.com/watch?v=4fk2prKnYnI
The Thrill is Gone

J esus! One side of my face was on fire, the flesh was disintegrating away, and my bones were pressing into the damp ground. The smell of burning stung my nostrils. Only when I brought my hands up in a panic to try to put the fire out did I realize that my skin was not burning. I looked at my hands in shock. Shards of sharp glass stuck to my palms and they were dripping with blood.

What the fuck!

Something *was* burning though.

Dazed, I turned my head. A few feet away my car was on fire. I watched it blaze towards the sky. Even in my disorientated state I could see how beautiful it was. Suddenly, I saw Stanley's face rise up from the seat. It was full of horror and his mouth was open in a scream of terror. I hadn't worn my seatbelt so the force of the crash had blasted me through the windscreen, but he was wearing his, and now he was trapped behind it and couldn't get out.

I had to get to him.

I tried to lift my body, but it wouldn't cooperate. As though I had turned to concrete. I couldn't feel anything. Not even the biting cold. I tried to crawl as excruciating pain ratcheted though my body, a hundred different places at once. A single cry bubbling up inside.

"Stanley!" The word tore from my throat. "Stanley!" I screamed and crawled onwards, grabbing at what I could of the glass and tarmac beneath my hands. He was saying something, but his face was bubbling and melting.

"God, no."

I filled my lungs with freezing air and went to drag myself up. It was like being stabbed in every part of my body, but not an inch could I move. Sweat poured out of my body as I pounded my hand on the ground in frustration. In agony, I watched the slight silhouette of the man who was more of a father than my own had been, collapse and fall out of view.

"This is a dream. Just a nightmare," a voice in my head screamed. I began to beat at my own body.

Wake up, wake up, Brett. Wake the fuck up. Now!

I jerked awake in the darkness of my room. Sweating, coughing, and clutching at my chest for dear life. I shot out of the bed, and such pain racked my entire back that my knees gave way underneath me. Grasping the bed, I stopped moving and stayed still, my teeth gritted. I just had to wait for the spasms to pass. They always did. I just had to be patient. To wait. The pain dulled to a bearable throb, but the dream remained vivid.

It would haunt me for the rest of my life.

Beads of sweat dotted my forehead, and misted on my chest from the nightmare. I glanced at the digital clock by my bedside. Only a few minutes past two in the morning. I had put myself to sleep barely forty-five minutes earlier. The thought of the long night still ahead made me groan quietly in misery.

With a sigh, I rose from the bed and hobbled over to the window. Seven months ago I was still crawling on my hands and knees to get to it, so this was progress, and I was grateful for that.

I opened it to allow the cool autumn wind in. Leaning against the pane I inhaled deeply, and tried to put the sickening images out of my mind. It was so still and quiet I could hear my heart beating. There was a wedge of moon in the sky. It cast its ghostly blue light on the flat wild landscape and made it seem magical. I closed my eyes and remembered the first time I saw this scenery. I could not connect with its raw untamed nature, or its complete isolation.

I was not a country boy. The hustle and bustle of the city was in my blood.

And yet I could not, not buy this fortress. Some primal instinct would not let me walk away from it so I acquired it. I imagined keeping it for a few years, then divesting it for a profit. Little did I know it would become a place where I would hide like a wounded animal from the world.

The revving of a car engine in the distance jarred me out of my thoughts.

I opened my eyes and looked out, past the massive iron gates. I watched a bright red Porsche zoom up the hill. One by one the two gates swung open, and the car pulled up at the courtyard below. The passenger door was pushed open, and a pair of glittery heels landed on the cobble stones. It was followed by long, ivory legs.

Then my wife of nearly a decade lifted herself out.

She looked stunning in a silvery mini-dress. Waves of silky long blonde hair blew in the slight breeze as an intoxicated laugh bubbled from her lips and rang out into the quiet night. I watched as the man at the driver's seat threw his door open and strolled over to her. He had dark hair, which he had slicked back, classic Mediterranean good looks. Dressed in an expensive suit. Something about the way he moved told me he'd never done an honest day's work in his life. His life was spent servicing rich, lonely women.

Slamming the passenger door shut behind my wife, he thrust her roughly against the sleek metal and she immediately raised her knees and opened her legs wide. He pushed his hand between her thighs and after a few seconds, thrust it upwards so violently, her head jerked back. In the moonlight her mouth was a dark O of shock and pleasure on her ivory face.

It seemed almost impossible to think of her as Stanley's only daughter, his Princess, the only real love of his life. He would have died for her. The day I married her, he cried and told me I had fulfilled his greatest dream.

The dark-haired man began to pump into her, fisting her so roughly it was as if he wanted to tear her apart, but her cries of pain mixed with pleasure rose like wings in the night air.

She'd finally found a man after her own heart.

CHAPTER 3

BRETT

I stepped away from the window, feeling nothing. My only irritation was the show had wiped away whatever slim chance I had of finding sleep again. I stood by the bed, my shoulders hunched. Life was only bearable because of one thing.

Only one soul would be able to call back peace into my heart.

Fitting my mask on to my face and pushing my arms through a robe, I exited my room. Silently, I made my way from my tower, which was also the highest and most inaccessible part of the castle, and went across to the main part of the house. It took only about five minutes to arrive at the corridor that lead to my son's room. I had just grabbed the handle of his door when the crashing sound in the hallway echoed in the empty silence of the great hall.

I let go of the handle and changed my destination.

Standing in the shadows at the top of the grand staircase, I saw my wife leaning against the wall, her body swayed as she tried to collect what remained of her senses. An antique bronze urn rolled on the floor.

Pushing herself away from the wall, she kicked off her shoes, before staggering her way towards the stairs. She climbed as though every step carried the risk of the ground giving way and sending her straight into a dark abyss. As I turned around to walk away, the movement alerted her and she swung her head in my direction. The shock of seeing me made her stumble backwards, her hands flailing, and just barely latching onto the banister at the last minute.

"Fuck!" she cursed, as she glared up at me.

I took another step towards my son's room.

"Wait!" she called.

I stopped and watched her dispassionately as she righted herself with some difficulty. When she was able to stand on her own she addressed me without a shred of shame or guilt.

"You almost scared me to death," she accused, one hand on her slender hip, and the other holding tightly to the railing for dear life.

"I can't remember the last time I saw you sober," I remarked.

She cocked her head and gazed at me in drunken contemplation. "I can't remember the last time I saw you without your mask."

I shifted my weight onto my other leg. It had started to throb. "How do you expect to care for Zackary if you're out getting drunk all night and asleep for most of the day?"

"You're a fine one to talk. At least I'm around for him." She staggered, but managed to catch herself in time. "But you're never around for him. He needs you too, you know?"

Her war of wit was infuriating and in her present condition any rebuttal would have been a pointless exercise, but I couldn't stop myself. "I would love to be around Zack, but as you are clearly aware, he's terrified of me."

"He's not the only fucking one," she muttered under her breath, but I'd heard it … as clear as day. A few years ago, it would have cut through my ego like a knife, but now it sifted through my consciousness like air. Inconsequential. I couldn't give a damn what she or anyone else thought.

"Get your act together," I said harshly. "Otherwise I'll step in." I whirled around to leave, but her words came after me, defiant and taunting.

"How dare you talk to me like that? I'm not your servant. I'm your wife, and the mother of your child."

"Then behave like one. Be a mother to that poor child."

"I have needs too," she cried.

"I am sure your needs are being met." My voice was cold and uncaring. The whole conversation bored me. All I wanted from her was to be a good mother to Zackary.

"What I need from you is a good fuck, but since you have relinquished even that basic duty, I'm forced to find other ways to keep myself alive. I know you saw what happened outside. Did you enjoy watching?"

I continued walking away, but at her next statement I screeched to a halt.

"I've hired a nanny if you care to know."

I turned slowly to face her. "What?"

"Of course, that would get your attention," she hurled. There was gloating triumph in her beautiful face.

"Why does Zackary need a nanny? Are you planning on going somewhere?" My voice was soft.

She raised her chin defiantly. "No, but I need the help. He's growing, just in case you haven't noticed. He requires more time and attention, and my life can't continue to simply revolve around him."

I thought of the dark-haired man with his fist inside her. "What then will your life revolve around?"

Her snort was bitter. "You've always been so condescending towards me. I'm nothing in your eyes, aren't I, Mr. Gazillion-aire. But you know what? You deserve the misfortune you've got. The only person who didn't was my father ... he got the brunt of your misfortune, didn't he? If my father saw the way you treat me now, he would turn in his grave."

She continued her ascent up the stairs, and I let her go past me. I did not trust myself to speak. I was furious at her crass mention of Stanley. How dare she say that? He had spoilt her rotten so she never knew real love for him. He was just there to pay for everything. If he was turning in his grave it would be because of how she had turned out.

"I'll keep myself and Zackary away from you, don't worry," she said. "The nanny will be here on Monday."

"Will she be residing here?" I asked from between clenched teeth.

"Of course, but don't worry, I'll be sure to warn her to stay away from you. You can just relay your instructions the same way you do with me. Through your esteemed intercom service."

"Goodnight *husband*," she said sarcastically as she passed, but then she stopped when she was at the entrance of the corridor to her wing. She glanced back at me, her face sly. "I wasn't joking earlier. I am drunk enough, but I wouldn't mind doing it once more for old time's sake? Your chill is just what I need to put me to sleep. Anyway, don't you want to know if your cock still works?"

Disgust pooled at the pit of my stomach. "Go to sleep, Jillian."

The mocking expression was suddenly gone and she just looked distraught. "Brett, remember when you used to come into my room while I was sleeping and just fuck me in the dark as if I wasn't your wife, but a total stranger. No words."

"That was eight years ago," I said harshly. "I was a different person then."

"I'm sorry. I was drunk. I didn't know what I was doing. Are you so perfect that you have never made a mistake?"

"You're wasting your time, Jillian."

"How many times must I say I'm sorry? I'm your wife, Brett. When are you going to treat me like I am?"

This was exactly the reason I didn't want to have this discussion while she was drunk. It was a waste of time. "You're my wife in name only. We have an agreement that benefits our son. The day it does not will be the day we no longer have our agreement. You do your part and I'll do mine."

"There's something missing in my life, Brett. I need you." She stood at the entrance to her wing, looking at me imploringly. At that moment, I almost pitied her. She was not happy, and no one could ever make her happy. I promised Stanley I would take care of her until my dying day and I would keep that promise, but that was all I was capable of doing.

Without another word, I turned and went to the wing opposite hers. Silently, I entered my son's room and stood looking down at him for a long time. Memories flooded into my head. Jillian announcing she was pregnant not to me, but at a dinner party in our home. She then proceeded to get so drunk she passed out before the last guest left.

The next morning, I took her to Switzerland.

She hated it, but there not a drop of alcohol was available for the rest of her pregnancy. Then, that moment of watching the top of Zackary's blond head appear between Jillian's legs. The wonder was indescribable, but it brought a feeling a new sense of vulnerability. For the first time in my life I was terrified. He was so small and helpless. What if I could not protect him?

The feeling never left. I felt it even now as I stood over him. Outside the wind had picked up and it howled around the turrets of the castle.

CHAPTER 4

CHARLOTTE

Though I was still very far away, the castle was already visible. Like a hulking, living monster shrouded in morning mist, it rose up from the ground and towered over the sleepy town in the valley below.

I stared at it in amazement. It was like looking at Saruman's castle. In the gentle light the gray stones looked dark, and forbidding, and nothing like the fairy tale, Sleeping Beauty, type castle I had spent almost a year in. I'd loved every minute of my time there and left with a heavy heart. Compared to this castle that one looked almost fake. I could almost have believed it, if someone had said this castle was built by Numenoreans, or magical ancient men from a vanished island.

As we got closer I could see there were two walls between the outside world and the castle. The taxi stopped in front of the solid iron gateway. The driver turned towards me, his eyebrows raised. "What do you want to do, Miss?"

"Give me a minute, please," I said and climbed out of the

black cab. The morning air was fresh and cool. I stretched my stiff limbs and walked over to a panel that looked like it could be some kind of intercom system.

I pressed the button and waited. A full minute must have passed and I looked around apologetically at the taxi driver, but he seemed to be no longer as impatient as he had been while we were still in London where he busied himself with roundly cursing and swearing at anyone who caused him to lose even a second of his time. He looked as awed by our surroundings as I was. I noticed the vertical sliding wooden grille shod with iron suspended in front of a gateway. In times of war or siege it was let down to protect the gate. Its sturdy design that was meant to repel intruders, but was actually at once brutal and strangely beautiful.

Just as I was thinking of putting my finger on the button and holding it there, a thickly accented, deep voice came through the speaker. For all I knew he could have been Count Dracula's butler.

"Yes."

I looked up towards the camera. "Er … I'm the new nanny, Miss Charlotte Conrad."

"Yes, you are expected. Come right up to the side of the house. There is a staff entrance there."

A mechanical growl sounded then, and nearly pulled my soul out of me. I jerked back as the heavy gates were pulled automatically apart. I felt a shiver go through me. It was a completely fanciful feeling, but I had the sudden and completely bizarre sensation that I wouldn't come back out the same if I went in. Shaking my head at my own silliness, I walked quickly up to the taxi, and got in.

"Are you going to be working here, then?" the taxi driver asked as we drove through the first gatehouse.

"Yes, that's right," I murmured, not taking my eyes off the frightening sight of murder holes in the ceiling high above us. Hundreds of years ago heated sand, lime, or boiling water would have been poured down on the enemies who had managed to breach the first defense. They suffered the cruel death of being roasted or boiled to death inside their metal armor.

Up ahead the second set of gates were opening inwards as if by magic. Surrounded by a moat we drove up towards the castle. It was easily the most impressive building I had seen in my life.

Two thick towers rose up on either side of the drawbridge. The gothic structure with its ramparts, arrow slits, bastions, battlements, timber corbels, and strangely beautiful crenelations, made me feel as though I had gone back in time to a lost and forgotten world.

The taxi came closer to the castle and I could see the massive front door was covered in iron studs, but I could also see a very much smaller door that was almost hidden away.

"Can you drive to that side, please?" I told the driver, pointing to the left.

The taxi came to a stop and I got out. The fare had already been paid in advance by April. She had insisted on it, because she knew I would have taken the train otherwise. He had not put the meter on, but I guess it must have run into the hundreds.

The driver smiled, his first of our four hours trip, wished me luck, and drove away. I walked over to the small door. It had a large lion-head knocker, but before I could use it the door opened and a balding, frighteningly thin man, attired in white gloves, a peculiar green vest, and a long-tailed charcoal morning coat, stood in front of me.

Wow! *A real-life butler* in full garb.

"I'm Barnaby Boothsworth," he introduced, his posture rigid and his eyes expressionless.

"Charlotte Conrad," I replied with a wry smile. "I guess I'm here to see Mrs. King."

"Of course." He stepped aside politely and waited for me to enter before closing the door and offering to take my suitcase directly up to my room. I handed my single piece of luggage to him and he led me down a dark corridor.

"Mrs. King will meet you in the drawing room," he said as he walked in front of me.

Just before we reached a wooden door, he stowed my suitcase into a nook in the corridor, then ushered me into a massive space.

Ah, the great hall.

Light flowed in through stained windows set high on the soaring walls. There was a humongous stone fireplace which I imagined in winter would heat up the entire room. A long wooden table that could seat about twenty chairs upholstered in green velvet stood in the middle of the room. Above it hung a truly massive chandelier. In a touch of almost poetic beauty, a magnificent marble sculpture of a centaur reaching his arms upwards had been placed in the middle of the table and underneath the chandelier, so it seemed as if the creature was reaching up to touch the light.

Large tapestries of hunting scenes decorated the walls. Green was the main color scheme of the décor here, and I understood then where the concept of his vest probably came from. It also gave me a look into the psychology of the mistress of the house, who had decided to match her servants attire with the furnishings. I suddenly recalled reading a book by a Victorian servant. He said the best servant was an invisible one.

Our shoes were loud on the flagstone floor as we crossed the great hall and made our way towards another room, which Mr. Boothsworth referred to as the drawing room.

"Please wait here," he said stiffly, before closing the door quietly behind him.

I looked around the room. The décor had obviously been executed by a professional decorator. It reminded me of watching a program on TV about a billionaire who was trying to sell his yacht to buy a bigger one. Its great selling point was everything in it was made from something unique that no one else had. The coffee table, for example, had been made from the skin of twenty-seven lizards, or something equally ridiculous.

Up on one wall was a lavish and very large painting of a beautiful woman with blonde hair. She was wearing a tiara and sitting on a large gold throne. A small, pale blond boy stood next to her, but he seemed almost ghostly compared to the vigor and greatness of the woman. I knew instantly I was looking at the portrait of my employer, Mrs. King.

Mesmerized by the splendor with which she had been

depicted, I walked closer to the painting and stared up at her. There was something about her eyes. The artist had captured something elusive. I couldn't quite put my finger on it, but I knew it would come to me. As I was trying to figure out the mysterious hidden message the painter had left for the viewer of his painting, the clack of high heels sounded outside. It stopped at the door.

CHAPTER 5

CHARLOTTE

Quickly, I moved away from the painting. Standing in the middle of the room I hurriedly adjusted my glasses and smoothed down my hair. A few seconds later the heavy door was pushed open and the woman in the painting stood in the doorway. The artist had not exaggerated her beauty.

I was certain she had to be in her mid-thirties, but she could have easily passed for my younger sister. She was speaking to someone on the phone, but the moment she sighted me, she locked her gaze with mine. I smiled politely and watched her take a seat, shapely legs crossed, the skin of her heels as smooth as a baby's, and the skirt of her deep pink suit riding high on flawless skin.

She took her time with the call, listening intently to what the person on the other end was saying, but her watchful eyes kept roving restlessly from my face to my body and back. I stood still and politely looked away. Finally, she ended the call which was clearly not important, but she did not want to interrupt on my behalf. It was a form of control. She wanted me to feel uncomfortable and establish her authority from the get go. She didn't know she hadn't made me feel uncomfortable at all. Every time people played such shallow games I just pitied them.

"Is it Charlotte?" she asked, her tone as smooth as honey, and eyes moving between my baggy dark pants to my ugly white jumper.

I smiled politely. "Yes."

"You don't look much like a Charlotte."

I knew it was an insult, but I was a professional. No way was I even going to recognize it as anything but an unnecessary comment. I let my smile widen. "I'm afraid that *is* my name."

"Yes." Her lips twisted into a cold, condescending smile. "I wanted someone with more experience, someone … older, but they told me you're the best."

"I try hard," I said quietly, looking unflinchingly into her eyes.

She raised one perfectly plucked eyebrow. "I suppose you'll do." She glanced at her slim watch. "I have a function to attend so I don't have all day. Let's get on with it." She pressed a button on a panel next to her chair. "Bring Zackary into the drawing room," she ordered, before refocusing her attention on me. "The housekeeper will show you around and fill you in on everything you need to know about how this household works: mealtimes, Zackary's schedule etc. However, all instructions pertaining to Zackary's education, or wellbeing will come only from me. Is that understood?"

"Yes."

"So whatever problems you encounter you are to bring it to me and only me. Is that absolutely clear?

I nodded. "Absolutely."

"The other thing you need to know is, Zackary's father lives in the South tower. He was involved in an accident three years ago that left him quite …" she searched for the words, "quite unsightly. As such he does not mix with the servants or the outside world. If you accidentally meet him while you are on your duties, please keep your head down and carry on as if you have not seen him."

I was sure my eyebrows had disappeared into my hairline. This was the weirdest thing I'd heard.

"If I am not around—sometimes I stay at our apartment in London—and some emergency arises, you will be able to speak to Zackary's father using the intercom system. You will find it has been installed in every room in this castle. Is that understood?"

"Yes."

She rose to her feet and headed over to a heavy, wooden desk in one corner. Slipping behind it she pulled out a sheaf of papers from one of the drawers. "Something else crucial to keep in mind; I am your employer, not my son's father so if you're given any instructions with regards to Zackary that is beyond the scope of what I have stipulated in these pages then you are to contact me first." Mrs. King held the stapled papers out to me. "Here you go. Let me know if anything is unclear or—"

I walked over and took them from her. "Thank you."

"Study them. They are very important."

"I will," I promised.

There was a polite knock on the door.

"Enter," Mrs. King instructed.

The door was pulled open and a well-dressed, little boy with a pale sickly face was led in by the housekeeper, a plump woman with salt and pepper hair and rosy cheeks. The moment the child saw his mother, he let go of the house-keeper's hand, and dashed over to her. She moved around the table to meet him.

At that moment, her phone began to ring so she used one hand to deal with it, while she used the other to lightly tap the tip of the little boy's nose. His lovely green eyes stared up adoringly at her. It was a strange thing to watch. The boy's utter devotion to his mother seemed bizarre, almost like something from a Victorian novel. He showed no curiosity about the presence of a stranger.

"I'll be there in half an hour," his mother said into the phone. "I'm just about to leave the house."

The boy rested his head against her skirt in a loving gesture and she lay her hand gently on his head, and I began to shift my earlier reservations about her. Maybe she did really love the child. Maybe I had been too judgmental. With the father effectively a hermit, the dynamics in the household had to be bizarre to say the least. My thoughts were interrupted by the sudden coughing fit that gripped the boy.

"What's the matter, darling?" Mrs. King asked.

Without warning, the boy jerked back and projectile-vomited. All over his mother's skirt. Her shrill shriek of horror almost made me jump out of my skin, and her instinctive reaction was to push him away from her.

My mouth fell open in shock as the boy fell on the rug and instantly burst into tears. The housekeeper didn't move, and when my disbelieving gaze found hers, she shook her head at me in a way, as if to warn me not to say anything.

"What are you doing standing there gawking at me? Can't you see that he needs you?" Mrs. King hurled at me.

Instantly, I sprang into action. Putting the set of instructions she'd given me on the table, I went over to him and picked him up. To my surprise, he stretched his arms upwards and went very quietly into my arms. I lifted him off the ground, he stared up at his mother through tear soaked eyes.

She had grabbed paper napkins from the desk behind her and was angrily scrubbing pointlessly at her skirt. "I'm already so late," she cried, as she gave up the exercise and looked in dismay at the stain. "Ugh ... and the smell. I have to change." She picked up her phone and, presumably began to call whoever she was meeting. Apparently, she had completely forgotten us.

"Come with me," the housekeeper said in a fierce whisper.

Carrying the boy, I followed her out of the room. His mother's curses faded in the distance as she led me down a dim corridor.

"I'm Mrs. Blackmore," she said over the sound of the child sobbing softly.

"And I'm Charlotte."

"Come this way, dear," she said, pulling open another door.

We had arrived in a very basic gray and white kitchen. All the luxury was for the mistress. Here only the servants worked.

"Stay with him. I'll go find a clean towel," she said and disappeared through another door.

I pulled out my handkerchief, lowered myself to my knees, and wiped the vomit off the side of his chin. I patted the tears off his face trying my best to console him but he wouldn't stop crying.

CHAPTER 6

CHARLOTTE

W hen Mrs. Blackmore returned, I looked at her. "Is he ill?'

She shook her head. "He's not ill, lass."

I looked at her curiously. "Why did he throw up?"

"He's just had lunch and got too excited about seeing his mother."

"Why should he get too excited about seeing his mother?"

"It's been a few days. Or perhaps he was just anxious." She lowered her voice to a whisper. "He's an incredibly timid child. Wouldn't say boo to a mouse."

I was irritated because I knew that even though she dropped her voice, he must have heard her critical opinion, so I pulled him into my arms and held him tightly, hoping my warmth would calm him down. A few seconds later he took one last sniff and wriggled in my arms. I let him go. He leaned back and stared into the eyes of the new stranger in his life.

"Hello, Zackary," I said brightly. "I'm Charlotte, your new nanny."

He watched me for a few moments as if trying to make up his mind about something, then to my surprise, he stepped away from me and ran back to the housekeeper and hid his face in her skirt. She made a face at me, but she looked down and gave him a sappy smile.

"Give the little lad some time and he'll get used to you," she said.

The dynamics of the house seemed very complicated, but I knew I could make the boy trust me. The sooner the better. I rose to my feet. "Perhaps a bit of exercise will do him some good. I'll take him out to the garden to play for a little while."

"Nooooo, you definitely can't do that," Mrs. Blackmore protested, her head shaking vigorously. She looked positively horrified.

"Why not?"

"You'll realize once you've read Madam's set of rules."

I remembered then I'd left my copy back in the drawing room.

Mrs. Blackmore filled me in. "Rule number sixteen. Zackary is not allowed to play outside."

I stared at her bewildered. That was the strangest thing I'd ever heard and I'd heard some strange things in my life. "Why ever not?"

"He's always been quite sickly so Madam worries about his health."

"But that's not enough reason for a child not to go outside to play. Sunshine and fresh air is a good thing for a growing boy."

"Madam sets the rules and they are not to be broken," Mrs. Blackmore said firmly, even though I could tell she secretly agreed with me.

I glanced down at the timid child as he watched me from beneath his curled elbow. Was this poor boy really a prisoner in this dark castle? No wonder he was pale and timid. The adults around him were scaring him half to death over everything. I wondered how I was going to get around this ridiculous rule. Another thought occurred to me. The 'rules' that Mrs. King had handed to me were at least eight pages thick. What other rules were there?

"Come on," Mrs. Blackmore said briskly. "I'll show you to his room. He needs to be washed and have his clothes changed." We left the kitchen and went up the narrow wooden stairs meant for servants. As our party ascended, it creaked at various points.

But once we got to the landing we were back in the grand part of the house as we passed another vividly painted portrait of Mrs. King. This time she was depicted as Cleopatra. The boy's room was the first one in the corridor of one of the wings. It was a room that had been painted as if the walls and ceiling were blue skies filled with fluffy clouds. Cartoon characters sat in their planes flying around us. Together Mrs. Blackmore and I washed Zackary and dressed him from his collection of formal clothes. Right after we had dressed him, he began to suck his thumb.

"That means he wants a nap," Mrs. Blackmore whispered.

She put him to bed, then we tip-toed out. After that she showed me to my room, which was just next door to Zackary's. There was a single bed and a cupboard in it.

"I had Heidi air it for you yesterday, but let's open the windows," she said. As she was showing me how the shower worked, we heard a car roar away.

"I guess that is Mrs. King going out, huh?" I said.

"No doubt."

"Okay, so just press that lever. That's easy enough. It seems very modern for such an old building."

"It's from the fourteenth century, but apparently, the master spent millions updating it. Plumbing, central heating. He even dug up the whole countryside to run high speed fiber cables to this area. He's some sort of big wig trader so he needs the internet a lot."

"Have you ever seen him? Mrs. King used the word unsightly to describe him."

Her face showed her disapproval. "I've talked to him on the intercom many times, but seen him only once. It was at night in the corridor. He had just left Zackary's room and was on his way back to his wing. He wears a mask on his face and there are some scars on his neck, but he is a fine man. Tall and broad with a full head of thick black hair."

"What happened to him?" I asked, my voice hushed.

CHAPTER 7

CHARLOTTE

"The poor man was in a car accident about three years ago. I think he was paralyzed for almost a year, but he fought back. He was in a wheelchair for another six months, but he wouldn't give up."

"Mrs. King said that if I was to accidentally run into him I was to pretend I had not seen him."

She sniffed. "You must decide for yourself what you want to do, but I wouldn't kick a man when he's down. There's nothing wrong with a polite greeting. He's not a monster. In all my dealings with him I found him to be fair and honest. And the man who comes in from the village four times a week to clean his wing says, he keeps to himself, but he never has a bad thing to say about anybody."

"I see," I said slowly. "What is the boy's relationship with his father like?"

She frowned. "I don't think they are ever together. Zackary's days are filled with activities that don't include his father."

"Why not?"

She sighed. "You must ask Madam that. She is the one who decides what happens in this household."

"What about the boy's relationship with his mother?"

"Oh, he just adores her. Worships the ground she walks on. You saw what he was like this afternoon."

"She must be a brilliant mother then," I said softly.

Mrs. Blackmore couldn't bring herself to agree. "She has her own life … her own plans … her own lovers …"

My eyes widened. "Really?"

"It's not for me to gossip or anything, but men come in from London and stay at the village bed and breakfast." She stopped and sniffed. "She visits them there. Once a month she will go to London herself and when she comes back, the other staff say, she has bruises all over her body. God only knows what she does there."

"What about Mr. King?"

"I assume he knows. She doesn't exactly hide it, coming back all hours of the night with slick men. It's none of my business, but honestly, no man should have to put up with it." She lowered her voice. "I suppose that is why they live completely separate lives. I have never, not even once, seen him and Madam together, not even to stay and talk in the same room. She occupies the East wing and he never leaves his quarters in the South."

At her words something heavy struck my heart. I didn't know who he was or the extent of damage that had been done, but I knew what disfigurement could do. It can completely ruin your life. When I was sixteen my friend had been the victim of an acid attack. Overnight her entire world changed. Her scars were so horrendous her own parents couldn't recognize her when the bandages came off. After years of surgery she was still a mess.

I used to fly into a rage whenever we went out together. All I wanted to do was confront the staring people and tell them to fucking stop staring, pointing, and whispering, that she was just a normal person with some scars, but I couldn't because then I would have called attention to and made it even worse for my friend. So I either glared at them, my eyes shooting sparks of fury, or I completely ignored them.

It was through her I learned how shallow and cruel the world can be. She didn't stand a chance. They rejected her purely on the basis of her looks. The depth of pain and abject despair she felt haunted her eyes and crushed her little heart. Sometimes she told me she wished she had not survived the attack.

In the summer we used to go and have breakfast picnics at the park. We'd go so early there would be hardly anyone there. At that time I was still living in my parents' house. One night she called me and asked me to come really early to her house. She said she had made my favorite double-chocolate cake. I was very greedy in those days so I left my mother's house at five. When I reached her house it was still in darkness. Surprised, I let myself in through the back door and crept up the stairs to her bedroom. I honestly thought she had overslept.

But Aisha was already stone cold in her bed.

On the bedside table was an empty bottle of pills and my

double-chocolate cake and two letters, one for me and the other for her parents. I didn't shout or scream. I sat on the bed beside her and read my letter. She apologized for the shock, but she knew I was strong, and I could help her parents by easing them into the news of her death.

After Mrs. Blackmore left I quickly went back to the drawing room and retrieved my notes. Taking off my glasses and releasing my hair from its tight bun, I lay on my bed and went through eight pages of closely typed instructions in growing disbelief.

The notes gave detailed instructions on every aspect of the child's life. From how the practice cards should be used to putting away project materials when projects were over. Even worse every single thing was regimented and tightly regulated.

Breakfast at 8.00, snack at 10.30, lunch at 1.00.

Not only the time of the meals, but what food and snacks could be had were detailed.

Only open the windows in the morning from 8.00am to 11.00am.

Do not allow Zackary to be outside.

Then …

Wear head coverings in the sun.

Which was it to be?

It was so ridiculous that by the time I reached the end I didn't know whether to laugh or cry.

I'm sorry, Mrs. King, but no. Just no.

CHAPTER 8

CHARLOTTE

I lay on the bed and stared at the ceiling. It concerned me now at how I would be able to navigate my way in a household that was so tightly controlled by what I would have deemed a psychopath. I wanted to help Zackary and perhaps his father too. I still felt a lingering sense of guilt about Aisha. I had not done enough for her. I should have known by her voice what she was planning to do. Maybe this was another opportunity for me to do for the father what I had not done for my friend. A second chance to redeem myself.

Maybe there was a reason I was here. But at the same time, I was not a person to suffer fools gladly. One of these days I was going to blow up and tell Mrs. King exactly what I thought of her and that would be bad, very bad for my resumé.

My phone rang. I got out of bed and accepting the call fell back into bed.

"Hey," April said. "How's it going?"

"I'm not sure." I twirled a piece of hair.

"What do you mean?"

"It's a weird situation."

"Weird like what?"

"Weird like the mother is a raving lunatic, the father has been in a terrible accident and has become a recluse that no one ever sees. The child vomited because he was too excited to see his mother. I've got eight pages of instructions from how to wipe his bum to how many grams of cereal he can get."

"Oh! My! God!"

I sighed. "That's what I thought."

"What are you going to do?"

"I don't know yet. I hate giving up before I even start."

"Don't think of it as giving up. You know I need you."

"Yeah, I know. But I can't walk away when things are so obviously wrong."

"You actually think you can help?"

"Yeah, I think I have a shot at the boy. He has spirit. It's a bit crushed, but I think I know how to make him come out of his shell."

"What about Godzilla though?"

"Actually, she doesn't look anything like Godzilla. The woman looks like she stepped out of a fashion magazine. She's very, very beautiful."

"It sounds like you have a keg of dynamite over there. You think you can handle her?"

"Depends."

"On what?"

"On how much time she actually spends here. It sounds like she spends a good bit of time out enjoying herself and hiring me I would take to mean she wants even more. I think I'll give it couple of days and see how things go. Now, enough about me, how are you feeling?"

"I'm fine. As a matter of fact, I'm feeling on top of the world."

"What are you doing?"

"I'm in bed."

I laughed. "I don't believe it. It's ten o'clock in the morning and you just had sex, didn't you? The amount of shaking you put your poor baby through it's going to think it's a bloody Martini."

"Very funny. Actually, we didn't have sex. Yuri just thought I needed to relax."

"OMG! He gave you a blowjob."

"He might have," she said smugly.

I smiled. "Remember the first day you came back after you met Yuri?"

"Yeah." Her voice was dreamy.

"Remember when I said I wanted to watch you guys have sex?"

"Yeah."

"I take it all back," I said dryly.

She just laughed shamelessly. There was a knock on my door so I told her I would call her back and went to open the door. Outside was a woman about my age.

She grinned widely at me. "Hi. I'm Melly. I'm Mrs. King's personal assistant and I just came to see how you are getting on. If you needed anything?"

I smiled back. It was good to see a genuinely friendly face. "I'm great. I haven't had a chance to look around or get a grip of my duties, but thanks for the offer. I really appreciate it."

Her grin widened. "Trust me when I tell you there isn't much going on. This has to be the most boring place on earth. There's one pizza joint in the village serving rubbery pizza. The library is full of old people smelling like sausages. The tea shop is nice enough. But the real saving grace is the pub. It's pretty dire most nights," her eyes twinkle, "but sometimes big brawny farmers come in."

I laughed.

"We should go for a drink some time. It'll be a laugh."

"Yeah, that would be nice."

"Okay, I'll give you a few days to get yourself settled in. I'm in the room by the kitchen. If you need anything just pop in and I'll be glad to help."

"Thank you, Melly."

"Right, back to the grindstone for me. I'll see you at lunch?"

"Yeah, sure. See you downstairs."

She flounced away, a bundle of joyful energy. I closed my door and leaned against it. Maybe I had been too hasty. If she could put up with Mrs. King and run such a happy ship, maybe I could too.

CHAPTER 9

BRETT

https://www.youtube.com/watch?v=kXYiU_JCYtU
Numb

I knew the nanny had arrived. I could not put my finger on it, but there was a subtle change in the energy of the household. At first I was against the idea, but I think I was wrong. A nanny would mean I no longer need to interact with Jillian to beg for information about Zackary. I could deal directly with the nanny. Every night I could call her on the intercom and ask for a breakdown of the day.

I worked all day long, but my mind wasn't on it.

I couldn't wait to talk to the woman and establish a good working relationship. Before Jillian poisoned her against me. I knew Jillian's methods. A drop of invisible poison at a time, daily. Drop. Drop. Drop. Until the victim is a dead man.

I didn't know what time to call, but when I had gone to visit my son last night, I had seen the room next to him had been aired and the door left open so I knew she was in the room next to Zackary. I could see his room from my quarters, which meant I could also see hers. I knew she would eat with the rest of the staff so I waited for her lights to come on. At half-past nine her light came on.

I had gone from paralyzed and broken in every sense of the word, to the present where a ray of light had filtered into my darkness. I clung to the hope that through her, little by little, I could ingratiate myself into my son's world until the day he became old enough not to fear me anymore.

I placed a call on the intercom system and waited for her response. She didn't answer immediately so I walked over to the window and I could see her shadow standing in the middle of the room. I wondered if she was still unaware of how the system worked. Then she walked forward and in a few seconds her voice came through.

"Mr. King?" she said. Her voice sent a shiver down my spine. It reminded me of being in a wood-paneled private room in a restaurant in France waiting for the waiter to uncork a 2003 bottle of Le Clos Du Mesnil. Listening to the sound of Krug gurgling into a glass. First the luxurious scent, then the dry taste of Krug on my tongue. Crisp bubbles breaking on my tongue, silky liquid running down my throat.

I found myself for a brief moment, unable to respond, to even speak. I couldn't understand the effect that one single word had on me. I knew she was most probably not beautiful and almost definitely a married older woman. Except for her PA, Jillian did not like young staff. Her reasoning was she liked experienced staff, but I think she hated any woman who was younger than her.

"Mr. King?" she called huskily.

I cleared my throat. It was a long time since I spoke to a woman and my voice sounded strange even to my own ears. "How is Zackary?"

"He's asleep. I put him to bed at the prescribed time, Sir."

"Please call me Brett."

There was a slight pause. "All right, Brett."

"What is your name?"

"Charlotte. Charlotte Conrad." She sounded young, but she couldn't be.

"How was his introduction to you?"

She sucked in her breath. For some weird reason I could almost picture her smile, pure and unrestrained. "He was quite shy at first, but as the day went on he became a bit more interactive."

"He is naturally very quiet," I said.

"Hmmm."

I could tell that she was uncomfortable, but I still did not want to let her go. "What was his day like?"

"Well, we had a strange introduction. He threw up."

"He threw up? Why? Is he alright?"

"He's not sick or anything. Mrs. Blackmore said that it was probably due to him being too excited to see his mother."

"Right." My heart sank. There was something unnatural and unhealthy about my son's attachment to his mother. He was too delicate, too afraid of everything. I was aware he needed a father figure.

"I was wondering—" She hesitated.

"Wondering what?"

"It's nothing," she replied.

"No, speak your mind."

"I just expected that a boy of his age would spend a lot of time playing outside the house. The weather was so lovely today, but of course, he is not allowed to play outside."

I frowned. "What do you mean by he is not allowed to play outside?"

For a few seconds she was quiet and I let the silence ride. I was getting to the bottom of this no matter what. "It's in my instructions. Zackary isn't allowed to play outside the house. I believe Madam may be concerned it would expose him to germs and diseases."

I felt the fury like a molten ball of lava in my gut, burning. I felt sick and my hand shook with my anger. Thank God, she was not in the castle. If she had been I feared I wouldn't have been able to control myself from going to her room and giving her a fucking thrashing she would never forget. But what would be the point, anyway? She'd probably get a sexual kick out of it. What the hell was she trying to do? What else was she doing without my knowledge? What other restrictions were in the nanny's list.

"Take him outside to play tomorrow," I said.

She took a deep breath.

"What is it?" I asked.

"Nothing," she responded. "I will do as you say tomorrow, Brett."

"Thank you," I said and cut the connection. For an hour I paced the floor. Then I called Logan, my personal assistant in London, and asked him to get me a bottle of Le Clos Du Mesnil.

"What year, Mr. King?"

"2003."

Two hours later I heard the helicopter land on the helipad. I waited fifteen minutes then I walked out of my bedroom. When the discreet knock came, I opened the door and Logan came in. The champagne was already inside an ice bucket and he had brought two flutes with him. He set everything on the table. "Would you like me to pour, Mr. King?"

"No, that will be fine, Logan. Thanks."

He nodded and left.

I sat in front of the window. The nanny's window was already dark. I lifted my glass in her direction. Things were going to change around here. I warned Jillian before. Our arrangement was only good while our son benefitted by it. She was sailing dangerously close to the edge.

I tipped the glass and let the bubbles break on my tongue. It was years since I last tasted it. Since I even wanted it. I didn't want that life back. I could see it clearly now. How shallow and meaningless it was.

I thought of Zackary's nanny sleeping peacefully in her bed and I wished her well. She had no idea she had woken me up from my deep sleep.

CHAPTER 10

CHARLOTTE

The sound of the helicopter blades woke me up from my sleep. I had dozed off after reading my book. I could hear it getting closer and closer and then landing. Without switching on my light, I walked over to the window, but it must have landed on the other side of the castle. The helicopter was switched off and calm was restored to the night. I looked at the time. It was nearly midnight.

I lay back down on the bed and wondered if someone had arrived. Seemed a weird time to be arriving. Then again it was a weird household. Perhaps it was Mrs. King coming back. I thought about my conversation with Brett King. His voice was deep and smooth. It sounded like the voice of a very sophisticated, suave man of great culture and knowledge.

Even though I had felt his anger throbbing through the intercom system his voice had remained incredibly calm. This was my first night in the country after a long time being in the city and I was struck by how incredibly quiet it was. I could literally hear myself breathe. The quiet was broken by my phone vibrating against the desk. I leapt out of bed. It was April. Taking it with me I plopped myself onto the bed.

"Are you still awake?" she asked.

I was instantly worried about her. "Yes, but why are you calling so late?"

"Why are you whispering?" she asked dropping her own voice.

"I don't know. It's so deathly quiet here, it feels wrong to disturb it."

She giggled. "You're mad."

"Tell me something I don't know. Come on, tell me why you're calling. Where is Yuri?"

"He's downstairs, working. After you told me about that weird household I couldn't sleep thinking about you. How did your first day go?"

I sighed and ran through my memories and impression of the day. They had all been inevitably overshadowed by my short conversation with Brett King.

"Oh Lord, what did she do?" she asked, thinking my sigh had been about Mrs. King.

"Nothing. She went to some function, probably in London, and hasn't come back yet. Unless, she was in the helicopter that just landed a few minutes ago."

"Then why did you sigh like that?"

"I just spoke to the boy's father over the intercom."

"Wow! What was he like?"

49

My mind went back to Brett's voice. "He was nice. He had a rich voice. One of those deep and smooth voices. I can imagine him wearing a velvet suit and sitting in a box in an opera house."

"I wonder if he was handsome?"

"I have no idea," I replied. "But he has something."

"What do you mean?"

"I can't describe it. There is something magnetic about him. I could listen to him all night."

"Whoa! Watch it. That's someone's husband, Charlotte." April sounded anxious.

"I didn't mean it in that way. I think I am attracted to him because he has suffered a lot and I want to try to help him. He loves his son, but the boy is afraid of him."

"Just be careful that it doesn't become anything more. Remember your motto. Other women's husbands are off limits."

"Yeah, I know that. I won't go there even though the house-keeper said his wife sort of abandoned him when he met with his accident and went her own way."

"Wow, she sounds like a complete bitch."

"Apparently, she has loads of lovers."

"You're not looking for an excuse to have an affair with him, are you?"

"Absolutely not," I said firmly. "I told you it's not like that. It's something to do with the guilt I feel about Aisha. I just think maybe I'm getting a second chance to help. To redeem myself."

She sighed. "It was not your fault, babe."

"I know. Look, I should go to bed. I'll call you tomorrow."

"Okay. Have fun indoors."

"No, I'm taking Zackary outside to play tomorrow."

"Hey! His mother said no."

"His father insisted otherwise."

"Whoa, Charlotte, you're on a tightrope right now."

"Tell me about it, but I have to do what's right for the kid. I'll just take him out for a short while."

"Alright then, let me know how it goes."

"Wait—" I called just before she hung up.

"What is it?"

"Does … can someone's voice affect you through the phone?"

She was quiet for a few moments, so I immediately stepped in. "Don't assume anything, it's just an innocent question."

"What exactly is innocent about that question? Whose voice affected you through the phone?"

"Goodnight!" I said to her.

But she was like a dog with a bone. "Don't you dare put the phone down."

"It's nothing, I was just wondering."

"Charlotte …"

I started to regret my decision to even ask the question in the first place. "You know who …" I mumbled.

"What? You just said …"

"Forget it. It's late and I'm tired."

Her voice was serious. "What was so special about his voice?"

I sighed. "I don't know. It was just … I'm not doing this. It was nothing. Goodnight, April."

I cut the call and threw my phone aside. I shut my eyes to sleep, but shivered at the waft of the early autumn breeze. The nights in the country were much colder than London.

Dragging myself off the bed, I headed over to the window by my bedside and was about to pull the curtains shut when I stopped. Mrs. Blackmore had told me earlier that his wing was opposite mine, across the inner courtyard. All the lights were turned off, other than perhaps one dim lamp, and I got the glimpse of a shadow by the window, standing silhouetted in the dark, just as I was.

I was startled, but I didn't scream in fright. Unmoving, I stood and watched the figure, tall and unidentifiable in the shadows for a few more seconds.

Was that him?

Whoever he was I knew he was watching me, staring straight ahead, and unmoving. I was suddenly hot. Stepping away from the windows I stood just inside the shadows and watched him. He turned away and I found my breathing was shallow. Had he truly been watching me, or was it all just my imagination? A trick of the light. My phone buzzed and I picked it up and smiled when I saw it was my mother trying to Skype me.

"I knew you were awake because I saw your green light," she said.

"You've really learned to use your phone properly now, haven't you?"

"Yes, I have," she said proudly.

I smiled. "Good."

"I didn't wake you, did I?" she asked.

"No, you didn't. How are you?"

"I'm alright. How are your new employers?"

"They're alright," I replied.

"Are they nice people?"

"Yeah, they're both great."

"Oh, good. You know how I worry about you."

"Mom, I'm living in a castle. You should see this place. It's like a fortress."

"Well, as long as they are nice to you."

"They are. I'm just about to go to bed, but I'll call you tomorrow, okay?"

"Yes, you do that. You must be tired. I just wanted to say thank you. I received the money you sent. You're a wonderful daughter to me."

Her compliment made my heart turn to mush. "Wow, you

change your tone so easily, don't you?"

"What do you mean?"

"Remember when you threw me down the stairs for being your too stubborn, bad tempered daughter?"

"I didn't throw you down the stairs, you brat, you fell."

"And whose fault was that?"

"I'm sending the money back to you if you're going to gloat about that accident," she snapped, and I was glad I had my feisty Mom back. "If not for those damn scraps they call a pension," she continued, "I wouldn't have to bother yo—"

"You're not bothering me, Mom. Being able to give back to you is a blessing for me. I love you."

She sighed deeply. "I love you, little one. Make sure you take care of yourself. When will your day off be?"

"I'm yet to sort it out. When I do I'll let you know, alright?"

"Very well, goodnight sweet child of mine."

"Goodnight, Mom."

CHAPTER 11

CHARLOTTE

I was very tired and deep in sleep, but I heard my door creak open.

My eyes fluttered open for a moment, but I saw nothing so I shut them and turned away, too exhausted to be bothered. Then, I felt the bed around me compress down as though someone were joining me on it. My heart lurched into my throat, and my eyes shot open. Through the darkness, I met the glittering gaze of a stranger.

A hand shot over my mouth to muffle the scream that rose up in my throat, but then I looked into his eyes and I knew he would not hurt me. He was wounded and I felt a simple peace settle over my heart.

I reached out a hand and touched his face. It was covered by a mask. It felt warm from his skin and it glinted in the soft shadows. He didn't do anything so I carefully took the mask off, but it was too dark to see his face properly. His eyes never left my face. My hand moved to the switch on the table lamp, but he caught it. His hand was large and strong. There were calluses on his palms.

What came next was a kiss. At first gentle, then more and more passionate until it shot a dose of ecstasy down to my core. My arms rose up. I found the fingers of one hand in his hair, and the other circling around his shoulders, as though terrified that he would disappear.

He dragged away his lips to press them on my neck. The action set me on fire. My arms fell away as I reveled in the sweet assault. An alarm sounded in the back of my head. *What are you doing, Charlotte? You don't know this man.* And yet I felt no real fear, or a sense of caution.

His hands tore away at my pajama bottoms. A gasp escaped my lips when the tip of his tongue dug into my navel. An ache began somewhere deep inside me. I began to writhe in anticipation. He opened my thighs and bent his head to look between them.

"Jesus, Charlotte. You're so beautiful. And so fucking wet," he rasped.

I recognized his voice and responded to it. He was no stranger. I knew this man.

He lowered his head I was still trying to see his face, but it was almost completely shadowed. When he took my swollen nub in his velvet mouth and sucked on it sensuously, like someone sucking a sweet, I almost shot out of the bed. Juices poured out of me.

My hands fisted the sheet and my body arched. The sheets were jerked out of their hold under the mattress when his hot, wet tongue lapped at me, as if I was a melting cone. I whimpered with ecstasy.

"Shhh … the child," he whispered, and clamped his hand over my mouth.

I couldn't recover, his tongue speared into me, and my hands tore at his hair.

My moans I was sure had moved to borderline screams. Thank God for his palm pressing down on my mouth. I tried to say something, but there was no coherence. Just a muffled animal sound. Weird. Embarrassing.

I wanted to come … I wanted this to end … before I went out of my mind.

My fingers moved to my swollen nub to aid the process along, but before I could get to it, he took it between his teeth and bit down. The pain was precise, but it was the trigger I needed. A scream was torn from my throat. Then, hot cream poured from my slit as I lost it.

"Fuck!" I cursed.

I had come, but the maddening ache for more refused to stop. I wanted more. Much more. Unsatisfied, I moved my legs and wrapped them around his head, trapping his mouth on my pussy.

Who was he? Who the fuck was he?

I needed to know. I needed to know now. I reached down to pull his head up to mine. It was too dark to see. I had to see his face in the light.

My hand was reaching for the light switch when I woke up.

I shot up from the bed, panting, sweat beaded across my forehead. The first weak rays of the morning sun were already pouring through my opened window. I looked down at myself in shock. My panties were drenched. The memory of the ache was still so poignant I shot my gaze around the room, certain that someone had been there, and between my legs.

I had never before had a dream that had felt so excruciatingly real. My core throbbed still. I glanced at the time on my phone and jumped up. Zackary's breakfast was scheduled for 8.00 a.m. sharp, but before then, the matter of a bath and the right attire for the first part of the day was needed.

It was already 7:30 a.m. I was off to a bad start.

CHAPTER 12

CHARLOTTE

Throwing my clothes on and without even taking a shower, I hurried over to Zackary's room. I found him still sound asleep. As gently as I could, I woke him up. He didn't seem surprised to see me, and actually gave me quite an angelic smile. As I was still practically a stranger to him, I thought he might cry or protest when I started to dress him, but he meekly stood still and allowed me to get on with it.

As a matter of fact, he hardly spoke.

A situation I found unnerving, because most children can't stop talking. They chatter incessantly, and are intensely curious about everything. On my first day at a job I am usually bombarded with all kinds of personal questions. Are you married? Have you got kids? Why? Don't you want kids, and on, and on.

Questions from Zackary? Nada.

He also hardly ever made eye contact. After a quick break-fast of toast and eggs, which he ate without any real appetite and almost mechanically, I decided that taking him to the garden would be no good. He needed mental stimulation. Possibly from other kids or a new environment. In my opinion there was nothing a good ride down a slide and a few tumbles in the sand perhaps with some other kids could not cure.

I asked Mrs. Blackmore if there was a playground in the village and her eyes nearly popped out of her head. Before she could open her mouth and remind me about the all-pervasive Instruction List, I told her I had spoken to Mr. King who had insisted that I take him out. I didn't tell her I only had permission to take him to the garden. Despite the look of fear, she arranged for us to be chauffeur-driven in an hour's time.

We got into a baby blue Rolls Royce. Some animation came into Zackary's face, not much, but I still considered it progress.

"Where are we going?"

"To the park," I said with a smile.

He turned his head and stared out of the car. As we passed an old-fashioned sweet shop I told the driver to stop. According to my list of do and don'ts all colored sweets were strictly off limits.

"Come on," I said, and despite the quiet look from the chauffeur, I took the child into the shop.

There was a bell on the door which tinkled as we walked into the shop. Even before the door had shut behind us our nostrils were filled with the sweet smell of sugar in all its forms. Zackary's eyes became as big as saucers. "I'm not allowed to eat sweets," he informed me gravely, "they're bad for me." His eyes begged me to say it was all right just this one time.

"You're not allowed to eat anything with preservatives, additives, and artificial colors," I said, "but we're going to have something." I winked. "Almost healthy."

For the first time since we met, his lips pulled upwards in a real, child's grin.

We left with a large lollipop made from organic juices and a bag of marshmallows that the lady assured me had no artificial colors or preservatives.

It was a small park and there were two mothers there with their children. They looked a bit younger than Zackary. To my surprise he refused to look at them. I took him down to the slides which were not being used. I was hoping the children would come and join us, but they didn't so I caught the eyes of the mothers and smiled at them. They smiled back. Zackary went down the slide three times then, he stopped and looked at me.

"I'm finished."

"Shall we go say hello to the other kids?"

"No."

I pushed the swing for him and he seemed to enjoy it a lot. When he had enough he simply said, "Thank you. I'm finished now."

I led him to the sand box, he seemed to be fascinated by the blue and red plastic molds. He began to build his own castle. When other kids came over to join him though, Zackary immediately rose up, and came to me.

"What is it? Don't you want to make friends?" I asked, but he wouldn't say a word. He just remained by my side and refused to join the others. He was way too timid for a five-year old boy. I knew he had a class with his reading tutor in an hour so we left.

I knew disobeying his mother would be trouble but I hoped that once she saw how her son had come out of his shell she would be happy or at least she won't be mad. Already I could see a slight improvement in his usually somber mood. The exercise in the fresh air had put color in his cheeks and given him an appetite. He gobbled up his lunch, amidst smiles from Mrs. Blackmore. Hopefully, his mother would notice his improvement and be more open to allowing him to socialize even more.

That was not the case however when a few hours later, she barged into his room. I was sorting out his laundry on the floor but quickly jumped to my feet at the dark fury in her face.

"You took Zackary to the park today," she barked, and at the annoyance on her face, my lips parted but no words would come out.

"Are you out of your tiny, uneducated mind?" she screamed. "Did you not read the instructions I gave to you?"

I felt anger flash through my veins, but I controlled myself. "I apologize, but you were not around this morning for me to check with you, but his father insisted that I allow him some play time outside today, especially since the weather was beautiful. I told him about your rule but he said that he would speak directly to you about it."

Something flashed in her eyes. Was it fear or something else?

Whatever it was it was primal and basic. "What did you say?" she asked, almost as if she was unwilling to believe me.

"Your husband insisted last night that I take Zackary … out."

Her eyes burned with dislike. She took a few steps closer, her gaze boring into mine. "Listen very carefully to me because I am not going to say this again. Obviously, you are still unclear about your position in this household. I am your employer, not my husband. I hired you. The contract is between me and your employment agency. Therefore, not only are the instructions I give you not to be so stupidly shared with him, but any instructions he insists on contrary to what I have laid out are to be reported first to me. I am in charge of Zackary, not his father. Have I made myself clear?"

For a second I wanted to argue back, but something made me hold my tongue. Something told me to step back. There was more at play here than her empty threats and fake anger. She was not livid because I had done something that could have endangered her child. She knew very well her list was bullshit. She was angry because I had spoken to her husband and communicated what any sane person knew. A child should be allowed to run free outside. She blinked and I realized that maybe, she was a little afraid of me too. Of what changes I could bring to the tightly controlled world of her child. Why she wanted it that way I didn't know yet. But I intended to find out.

"Yes," I said slowly. "You have made yourself very clear."

"The next time you do cross the line your bags will be out on the street," she said to me, before turning on her heels and stalking away.

I turned around and Zackary was standing behind me. His

eyes were wide and he was shaking with fear. Walking over to him, I got on my knees, and gathered him close to my chest.

"Oh, darling. Don't be afraid. Everything is going to be fine," I whispered. I could feel his heart thudding fast and loud.

No matter what happened I wasn't going to abandon this child until I had made it clear to his father that he had to involve himself in his son's life, or the boy's life was going to be ruined.

CHAPTER 13

BRETT

How odd? I had kept myself busy with work all day long, but secretly a part of me had waited to hear her voice. It flowed into my ear like warm honey, and yet what she was saying crushed my heart. "He was timid around other kids?" I asked, frowning.

"Yes, he was," she responded. "The moment they tried to join him he stood up and came to me without a word."

"Why did he do that? Did he seem nervous?"

"I don't know why, but he does always seem to be on guard, as though he is afraid of something, or expecting to be spooked."

"Maybe he has been spending too much time in the house, perhaps more visits like this would help to bring him out of his shell."

She went quiet.

"What's wrong?"

"I was told by Madam this afternoon I can no longer take Zackary out of the castle. Also, I am no longer allowed to take any instructions from you. I am to report only to her … I will lose my job if I disobey her."

I cursed myself for not dealing with Jillian earlier. I could see the battle lines had already been drawn with Charlotte. "I'm sorry you have been put in such an awkward position. The fault is mine. I should have spoken to her as soon as she got back from London."

"It's okay. I understand."

"You *will* take him out tomorrow. He is in your care now. I should be able to trust that at all times you will look out for his welfare and only his welfare … without apology or reservation."

"You can absolutely depend on that," she responded. "If it makes you feel any better, Brett, children look small and fragile, but they are extremely resilient. Nothing hurts them for long."

I smiled slightly. Suddenly I had a memory of Zackary when he first started walking. He tumbled and fell backwards. The sound of his head hitting the wooden floor was so loud I swear I lost ten years of my life thinking he'd either cracked his skull or suffered brain damage, but other than a few tears there was no lasting damage. "Thank you for telling me that. I appreciate it. I suppose you have a lot of experience with children."

She laughed, a warm, beautiful sound.

"I'll speak to his mother tonight and sort the problem out,

but if you have any issues at all call me immediately using the telecom system."

"One more thing before you go …" she began.

"Yes?"

"There is not much that is interesting for Zackary to do here. He enjoyed playing on the swing and the slide at the playground. Would it be possible to have a swing set, a slide, or a trampoline installed on the grounds for him?"

"Of course. That's a brilliant idea. Well done. I have no experience with children so feel free to suggest anything else you feel will be useful for my son."

She hesitated.

"What is it?" I prompted.

"Uh, playing with his father would also be of great help. I don't know how possible that would be, but your presence sometimes would do him a world of good."

Her words were like a blow in the gut. There was nothing in the world I would have loved or cherished more, but it was impossible. Not while Zackary was terrified of me. I knew something had to be done, but until Charlotte came into the picture I didn't know what. I was paralyzed with fear I would make it worse, but I could see a ray of light at the end of the tunnel now and I had already started walking towards it. "Perhaps one day," I said softly. "I'll call again tomorrow. Goodnight, Charlotte."

I pulled out my phone. Jillian was on the line in moments. "Hello, Brett."

"I need to talk to you. Now," I said.

She snorted. "Oh, I'm sorry, but this lap dog is not at home now."

"You better be here before the hour is up or I leave you without a dime to your name."

I hung up the phone before she could say anything else. Then I opened my desktop computer and got to work assessing the project Logan had just sent through. Just before the hour struck, I heard her heels on the stone floor outside my door. I sat back as she strolled into my study. She was furious, but she smiled coldly.

I didn't smile back. "Why have you restricted Zackary from playing outside?" I asked.

She threw her purse onto my desk in annoyance. I kept my gaze on her, but ensured I remained calm.

"Since when did you start butting into my parental charge of Zackary?"

I lifted my gaze to hers. "You told me to leave him to you for the time being. You told me you would slowly bring him out of his shell, but if stifling the child is your special method I'm going to have to withdraw that right."

Her face instantly hardened. "Don't you dare," she hurled to me. "I'm not stifling him. You said it yourself, a child needs his mother."

"Not when she seems to be doing more harm than good."

She looked at me incredulously. "It seems the nanny has pledged her allegiance to you. Tell me, what did you offer her?"

I frowned. I didn't want this to be about the nanny. If we

carried on this vein the nanny would be gone in no time. "She has not pledged her allegiance to me. She has nothing to do with this. She simply told me you had instructed her not to take Zackary out when I suggested she do so. Was she lying?" I looked at her sternly.

She sighed. "Just back off, Brett. I know what I am doing. You'll do Zackary more harm than good. I'm his mother. I know what's best for *my* son. Just stay away," she said, "and leave him to me for now."

"Give your permission to the nanny to let *our* son engage in outdoor activities, otherwise I'll personally step in." My voice was pure ice.

She held my gaze boldly until she realized I meant every word. Snatching her purse from the table, she rounded on me. "How long are we going to keep this up?"

"Keep what up?"

She glared at me as though I betrayed her, but we both knew what the truth was. "Are we married?"

"What's your point?"

"You see me go out at night … you know exactly what I'm up to. That I fuck other guys. And yet you say nothing. Don't you care?"

I smiled cynically. I would have to be a complete fool to believe she was doing it to get my attention. "Were you doing all that to get a response out of me?"

"What man who claims to love his wife wouldn't respond?"

"I've never claimed to love you, Jillian," I corrected her. "You knew the score from day one. I married you because your father asked me to. I owed my life to him and he had never asked me for anything else, and you were not exactly ugly so I agreed. But as of now the only glue between us is Zackary. If at any point you get tired of your life here and want to leave, there's nothing holding you back ... but Zackary stays."

"You think he would want to live with you?" she challenged.

I felt the blood drain from my face. This woman knew which buttons to press, but my voice was even and calm. "Why? You think he wouldn't want to because of my scars?"

"Have you forgotten, he's terrified of you."

It hurt to hear it, but I pretended to chuckle. "So you've said, but he won't be five forever. One day he will understand."

"Maybe one day he will, but he needs me now. You've seen how attached he is to me."

"When was the last time you fed him, hugged him, or even spoke to him?"

"My father would have been so disappointed in yo—" she began.

Fury rose up in me like an out of control forest fire. I couldn't control the emotions that swarmed into me at the mention of her father. Until Zackary was born he was the only person I had truly loved. It killed me to see her use him to try to make me feel guilty. "Don't you dare mention him," I warned through gritted teeth. "The only reason you're still here is because of him. Never forget that." Unable to stand another second of her vile presence I rose to my feet and ordered her out.

CHAPTER 14

CHARLOTTE

D inner with the rest of the household staff was, as usual, a jolly affair. They were a good lot, without airs and graces and after just two nights they had already accepted me as one of the team.

Even though Mr. Boothsworth looked like a corpse warmed over, he had a dry and clever wit that made me warm to him the most. The Chef had more than enough stories of his escapades with women in the past to shock us all, and Mrs. Blackmore's snappy side was brought to life every single time the Chef opened his mouth. I was starting to think there might be some kind of chemistry growing between them.

Once Melly whispered to me that there was talk that there had been something between Mr. Boothsworth and Mrs. Blackmore in the past. The thought, though amusing, was a little bit disconcerting too. I couldn't imagine a more unsuitable couple.

It was late when we ended our meals and headed off to retire to our various sections of the house. As Carrie, one of the maids, and I were about to part ways at the top of the stairs, I couldn't stop myself from asking, as innocently as I could, "I heard you've worked here a bit longer than Mrs. Blackmore."

"I have," she replied. "Three years now."

"Have you ever seen Zackary's father?"

"No, nobody has seen him," she said.

"Oh." I tried my best not to show my disappointment.

"But I did find a picture of him … it was definitely before the accident since there were absolutely no scars on his face."

"Where is it?" I asked. "Could you show it to me?"

She looked around for a moment before returning her gaze back to me. "I can, but … it would be a rather dangerous mission."

"What do you mean?"

"It's in Madam's room. She keeps a framed picture of him hidden in her dresser."

My mouth opened in comprehension. "Ah …"

Carrie nodded meaningfully. "It makes me think sometimes that maybe she still loves him, and her messing around is all an act, but I don't know what to think when it comes to this household."

"Will you show me the photo?"

She looked doubtful. "I don't know I'd have to smuggle it out and …"

"Where is her room?"

"She used to be in the big room next to Zackary's, but she moved to the East wing last year since she kept waking the boy up with all her noise."

"Why not just take me there now?"

Carrie glanced at her watch. "Now might not be a good time …"

"She just went out an hour ago. It'll be ages before she gets back," I said hopefully.

"True, but what if she comes back?"

"It'll only be for a second and we can hear the car come up the road anyway," I coaxed persuasively. "We'll be out in no time."

With a sigh, she made a gesture with her hand to indicate I should follow her. We hurried up the staircase. Mrs. King's room was every bit as grand as I had expected. It was decorated in white from her curtains to her beddings, and then with accents of a deep red in the vase of roses that sat by the corner and the settee by the window.

"See that pure white bedspread," Carrie said as we hurried over to a French style dresser on the other side of the room.

I looked over to the bed. It was covered in white fur. "Yeah?"

"It's made from the white bellies of little squirrels. Hundreds of them."

"Ugh."

"It's in here," Carrie said, as she dug through one of the bottom drawers, and produced a small framed photo of a man with thick dark hair and gray eyes.

I felt my breathing stop.

I stared at it, unable to speak, and didn't even know that I had taken the picture from Carrie and was holding it in my hand. In the photo he was laughing, a drink in one hand, and the other across the top of the bench he was sitting on. I wondered where it was taken and just how much of this man his accident had killed?

"He's a handsome devil, isn't he?"

"Are you sure this is him and not one of her lovers?" I asked, raising my head to look at her.

Carrie pulled a face. "Hmm ... I never thought about that. Oh well, maybe it's not him then."

With one last look at one of the most intensely handsome men I had ever seen in my life, I gave the picture back to her and watched as she quickly returned it to the drawer.

For some reason I found tears in my eyes and before Carrie could notice them I turned away. But the voice did indeed fit perfectly with the man: calm, and seemingly larger than life. At least that part of him had remained.

"We need to leave now," Carrie said. I nodded in agreement.

We exited the room and parted ways. I returned to my room. The room was filled with beautiful blue light from the moon. I love moonlight so without switching on the lights I put the baby monitor on my bedside table, took off my glasses, and released my hair from its tight bun. Lost in thought I walked to the bathroom. Unzipping my unglamorous dress, I dropped it into the wash basket.

Then, I switched on the bathroom light and ran the bath. I

came back into my room in my underwear to get my book. I picked it up from the bedside table and was suddenly aware of a movement by the window.

I couldn't stop the startled scream that jumped out of my throat. The curtains moved and Mrs. King took a step forward. There was something menacing about her. Something mad. This woman was dangerous.

"I …What—," I began. I was shocked to find her in my room.

"Lose the stuttering," she said calmly to me.

Her calmness had a strange effect on me. I was suddenly keenly aware and completely calm too. I was at a disadvantage in my underwear, but I was not afraid of her. "What are you doing in my room?"

"Shouldn't I be asking what you were doing in mine?"

I felt the first frisson of fear. She must have seen us come out of the room, or more likely go into it. "I'm sorry. I didn't think you would mind. I was just making sure I knew where it was in case I needed to get there in an emergency."

"Mmmm."

"Did you want something from me, Madam?"

She stepped closer and the light from the bathroom fell on her face. I was convinced then, that she was truly dangerous. "You're quite the telecaster, aren't you?"

"I'm sorry. I don't understand."

"Are you trying to drive a wedge between me and my husband, little fat girl?"

My mouth opened in shock, but before I could say a thing, she interrupted me.

"Save it," she snarled. "From now on you can take Zackary out to play, but only after his tutoring sessions. Thereafter you must wash him down meticulously and ensure that he is spotless. Make sure his fingernails are clean. Do you understand?"

"Yes," I responded automatically. Being caught off guard in my underwear had robbed me of my confidence. I just wanted her out of my room.

"You better keep your eye on him and immediately report any scrapes or accidents. If he gets sick you'll have to answer to me."

"Yes, Madam."

"Remember," she took a step closer to me.

She was so malignant I had to resist the instinctive human impulse to step back from danger.

"One false move and you're out of here." Throwing a last triumphant look at me she sauntered out of the room. The door closed. I could still hear the water running in the bath-tub. Soon it would be full.

I knew I should go and turn the taps off, but I just stood there shaking with a combination of shock and fury. I knew I had fat thighs, but … Shit. What a bitch. No one had ever spoken to me like that in my life. If anyone had dared I would have fought back, and told them to fuck off.

I should have fought back. I'd always been a fighter, I couldn't understand why I didn't. I was no coward. I should pack my bags and get the hell out of this mad-house. I knew I should. I had unknowingly stepped into a viper's nest. It wouldn't be quitting if I did. Anyone could see the best thing to do in this situation was to get the hell out as soon as possible. It was a lost cause. If I told April she would send her husband's helicopter to come get me, but I couldn't.

I just couldn't.

I walked to the door and locked it. After that I headed towards the bathroom. Turning off the taps, I took the rest of my clothes off and got into the warm water. Silky water swirled around my thighs. I stroked them slowly as if they had feelings and she had hurt them. My mind was blank. I didn't understand why I had allowed her to get away with talking to me like that. Why it was so important for me to stay. Was it because of the boy, the father, or because I knew she had declared war? She had deliberately come into my room and acted like she was a mad and dangerous foe to frighten the living daylights out of me. She expected me to leave after this.

But not so fast, Madam. I don't scare that easily. I wasn't going anywhere. Not yet, anyway.

I got out of the tub, and naked, walked over to the window. Clouds had obscured the moon, but there were a great many twinkling stars in the sky, but my eyes looked for only one thing in the darkness. The lights in the room facing me were turned off, and I wished more than anything that he would appear in the window just like I had been certain he had on my first night here.

There was no sight of him and no call on the intercom either so I got into my pajamas and slipped into bed. The last thing

I thought of before falling asleep was not the way Mrs. King had humiliated me, or how pathetic she had made me feel, but of a mysterious man with gray eyes, and how his beautiful eyes had remained passionate and intense, even though he was caught in a moment of laughter.

CHAPTER 15

CHARLOTTE

I awoke with a renewed sense of purpose. I had a job to do. I was going to do it to the best of my ability. As stipulated by his mother in the memorandum of his care, I primped Zackary to perfection. One day soon I was going to stop this nonsense and teach him to dress himself. It was ridiculous that a child his age couldn't dress himself.

His little socks matching his tie and his blond hair combed back neatly, we went to breakfast. I watched as he solemnly ate up Tuesday's breakfast (scrambled eggs and homemade sausages), and was quite struck at the lack of resemblance between him and his father.

He was wearing a ridiculous stark white dress shirt which I couldn't help but secretly hope he would ruin by the end of the day, and a pair of dark slacks that I was sure had had more care given to its tailoring and fit than even my most precious outfit.

He looked stiff and uncomfortable, even as he ate, his gaze restlessly moving and watching the transfer of food between his plate and lips. Poor kid was on lookout for stains on his clothes.

Before I could stop myself, I reached out and ruffled his hair. He looked up at me, surprised and questioning. I grinned at him. He didn't return the grin. Placing his fork down, he smoothed his stubby fingers through his hair and sleeked it all back in place. Then he reached for the napkin on his lap, wiped his hands, and continued with his meal without ceremony.

I caught Mrs. Blackmore's gaze and she shrugged and gave me a glum look.

"Zackary, we'll be going out to play today," I said to him. "Are you excited? I think you'll have an amazing time."

"I'm not allowed to play outside," he responded.

"But we played outside yesterday. Didn't you enjoy it?"

"It upset Mummy." He shook his head before lifting his glass of freshly squeezed organic orange juice for a sip. "I don't want to anymore. I'll get dirty and there are creepy crawlies in the grass."

"Mummy said you could," I quickly clarified before he ruined such a prospective day for me. "She visited my room last night and said I could take you out for a little while."

The way he watched me was too controlled for a five-year old. "She did?"

"Yes, Master Zackary." I whipped out the most matron-ish voice I had. "She absolutely did. And as for creepy-crawlies. Do you know what I used to do to them when I was your age?"

"What?" he asked, big eyed.

"We used to catch them in matchboxes and feed them to my pet bird."

"What kind of bird was it?" he asked, intrigued in spite of himself.

"A baby sparrow. It had fallen out of its nest and my friend and I rescued it."

"Where is it now?"

Of course, it was dead. Nearly twenty years had passed since I fed Billy Face with worms and insects I had caught. "I don't know. One day when it had grown bigger and stronger it flew away."

"Do you think we might find a baby sparrow too?" he asked hopefully.

I smiled. "Maybe, but we have to be out and about to do that."

"Okay." He smiled shyly back at me and I felt a surge of happiness. What a beautiful, but careful soul he was. My goal from then on became to unwind him as much as I could before my time as his nanny came to an end. I knew without doubt that I had very little time left too.

He returned his attention to his meal, while I discreetly pulled away a blade of his hair to lessen the polish that I had taken such pain to attend to earlier in the morning.

"Where do you plan on taking him?" Mrs. Blackmore asked me.

"Today we'll spend it on the grounds," I replied. "Maybe next time we will visit the park again."

"The grounds are empty," she reminded me. "Are you both just going to play with the grass?"

I grinned at her snappy question. "No. I'll run out to the store for some makeshift supplies until he gets his proper playground installed."

"Oh, he's getting a playground, is he?"

"That's what his dad said." I turned to look at Zackary, but once again he had lost interest and was concentrating on eating without soiling his clothes.

"Are you taking the little one with you?" Mrs. Blackmore asked.

"Of course. He can help me choose the stuff he wants."

"That's a good idea, love. He's never been to one before. There's a big new American style store a few minutes away."

"Yes, I know. I googled it this morning."

In half-an-hour we were in Bright Buy. I chose a huge cart despite not needing much so that he could ride in it, but when I asked if he wanted to ride inside he had looked at me as though I were out of my mind. When I glanced behind I met the carefully blank look from the suit and tie bodyguard/chauffer Henry.

I shrugged. You couldn't say I didn't try.

On my way to the crafts aisle I passed by the toys area to see what he would be drawn to, but he just walked past everything with a look of great disdain. As if toys were beneath him.

As we made our way through the aisles we came across other

kids sitting amongst produce in the carts and being pushed around by their parents, and one little girl who was writhing in tears on the floor obviously to protest her mother's behavior. That was the good and bad of child behavior, but the child beside me watched them as though they were all nothing but uncivilized lesser mortals.

Our roles almost switched when we arrived at the arts and crafts aisle. I found quite a few things that I wanted to check out and Zackary kept up his disinterested attitude. I didn't let it bother me. As I picked this and that, I could see his interest slowly peaking. When I put two bundles of string into the cart, he could no longer hold his curiosity.

"What are you going to make, Miss Conrad?"

"Not me. *We* are making a kite," I said.

CHAPTER 16

CHARLOTTE

With my supplies stashed away in the boot, I took on a crash course on how to build a kite on You Tube on the way home.

When we got in I scattered the materials on the floor of the great hall and began opening all the packages. I had the sticks in hand and was ready to begin when I met Zackary just watching me, a frown on his face. I felt a bit guilty then as though I was the one sourcing the most entertainment from this.

"You have to help me make the kite," I said to him.

"It's dirty on the floor," he said.

"It's not. Frances just cleaned it this morning."

He looked at me doubtfully and I wondered how long it would be before I got him to act like a child, less concerned with dirt than play.

"I tell you what. If we get our hands and clothes a little dirty, we'll just quickly go upstairs and have a bath before lunch."

"What if Mummy sees me?"

"She's out. She sent me a text that she will be back after lunch."

Before he could think about it too hard, I jumped up and pulled him down beside me. And so we began our first project together. Zackary helped out as I instructed him to and the time went by like a dream. A little while later, our simple kite was done and stood crooked and gloriously frail against the ancient walls.

But Zackary was not ashamed of the messy contraption we had made. His smile stretched into a full grin and his eyes shone with pride and appreciation. For a moment he looked the way a little boy should again. I just prayed it would fly, even if for only a few seconds.

Zackary turned to me excitedly. "Do we fly it now?"

"Uh, not yet," I replied, drawing the remaining bag of supplies towards me. I retrieved some paint and brushes, and laid them all out before him. "You have to make it pretty first."

"Why?" he asked genuinely clueless. Now he was sounding more and more like a little boy.

"We have to paint the kite and take a picture for your parents. They won't be very impressed with such a plain kite."

I laid out some colors for him on the palette and then handed him the brush.

"What do I paint?" he asked, his forehead crinkling with a new anxiety.

"Hey?" I said, placing my hand upon his. "Are you nervous?"

He nodded.

"Why?"

He turned to gaze at the blank kite. "I want my mummy to like it."

"Ah," I understood then.

"This is your kite, so paint whatever you wish on it."

But that only served to paralyze him more. It was clear how desperately he needed his mother's approval.

I knew I had to do something to break the impasse. Perhaps if I stimulated his over-developed need not to act like a child. I reached forward and whispered in his ear, "Should we just splatter paint all over it? Maybe just dip your hands in paint and plop it all over —"

"Finger painting is for babies,' he said scornfully.

I held both of my hands up in defeat. "Yes, Sir."

I laid the kite on the ground and watched as he lowered his head and got to work. I paid close attention and a little while later could see the picture as it began to form in a corner. At first was the sun. A bright yellow circle with precise strokes coming out of it, then green blades of grass which he meticulously and carefully filled half the kite with. On the second half of the still blank space he painted a small round face with a stick body.

He gave himself a swirl of yellow hair, and then moved on to his mother. She was also a stick figure but for her legs, he thought in the last moment to dot with a blob of red representing her shoes. He did the same to her lips while her blonde hair received the same yellow swirls as his had done.

I thought he would stop there but then some distance apart he began to draw an even taller figure. My heartbeat slowed down as I watched silently. He painted two black blobs for his shoes, but then he kept going with the brush and painted his father's face black.

"Why?" I turned to him. "Why did you paint his face black? I can't even see his lips."

"It's a mask," he stated quietly, as he dipped his brush in white paint. With it he marked a smile across the black face. He made a startled sound when the paint smudged and looked up at me in confusion.

"That's easily fixed," I said and took the brush from him. I scraped the white away, repainted the face black and gave the brush back to him. With his little tongue poking out of his mouth he carefully added another white smile on to his father's black mask. Then to my surprise he used the brush to connect his tiny stick hand with that of his father. He smiled up at me, to announce the completion of his task.

"Your dad is holding your hand?" I said.

He nodded. "I haven't seen him for a very long time. Mummy says he is very busy."

"Do you miss him, Zackary?"

His answer surprised me. "He makes me cry."

He rose to his feet then, lifting the kite up and handed it over to me.

We put it away to dry and I reached for the water balloons.

The next twenty minutes were spent filling them up by the tap. By the time we were done he was already half soaked, his cheeks rosy from all the laughing at his struggle in tying up the balloons without the water spilling out.

"We need a songstress," I said.

"What's a songstress?"

"Someone who can sing."

"You can't?"

I puffed up my chest and spurts of laughter escaped my throat. "Well, I mean, I'm not too bad."

"Go on then. Sing something," he urged.

I waved my hand as though there were a crowd waiting just holding their breaths to listen to me and bless them with my talent. Zackary just stared at me curiously.

"London bridge—" I screeched.

"Nooooo," he screamed, his hands flying to his ears.

My eyes nearly popped out of my sockets. "Your voice can get that loud?"

He started giggling then.

"You sing then." I pulled the bucket of balloons towards us. "We'll pass this between us and when the song stops the person who's holding it, will get a balloon squashed on their heads."

He squealed with excitement at the prospect of squashing balloons on my head, and once again I was taken aback by how completely different he had become in the space of one morning.

"I'll start," he yelled and began to sing Baa, baa, black sheep.

I considered letting him win the first round, but since he'd never squashed a balloon on anyone's head before it would be safer if I won the first round and let him see how it is done. So with more excitement than I should have had, I squashed the neon green ball on his head. It drenched him all the way down to his clothes. His laughter rang out to the skies, and his eyes sparkled with glee. I let him win the next round and he was brutal with that balloon.

We kept at it until we were both soaked to the skin.

"Come on," I said taking his hand. We headed out to the garden to pass the balls between ourselves. "Whoever lets it drop will be blasted."

We played until we abandoned the game all together, and it turned into a full out balloon fight.

We ended sprawled on the grass, exhausted. There were pieces of blasted rubber all over the grass. "Are you cold?" I asked him.

"No," he said, but I could see he was.

"Come on, let's get you in the bath. We rose up and found to our surprise the entire staff had gathered by the door to watch us, amusement all over their faces.

"We took pictures," Carrie yelled out.

"Take this one." I yelled back and lifted Zackary as far up in the air as high as I could. He yelped in startled joy, his legs flailing.

The shot captured was pure perfection.

CHAPTER 17

BRETT

This was the first time I had traveled to London, or for that matter, anywhere, ever since I left the hospital, but it had worked out well. I only met with Logan and worked on a new investment projection alone, but it still felt good to leave the castle. Even my back didn't hurt. I ran my hand along the large raised scar on my thigh. Actually, even my leg was feeling a lot stronger. Though I'd had a long day it did not throb or ache.

Perhaps all my pain was in my mind.

By the time I arrived home it was nearly midnight. The first thing I did was pull apart my drapes to see if Charlotte's light was still on. It wasn't, but the little bedside lamp in Zackary's room must have been on, because its greenish light filled his window.

I frowned. Surely, he was not still awake at this time.

I picked up my phone and called Barnaby to ask him to go check on Zackary. But as if on cue, the light in Zackary's room went off and seconds later the light came on in her room. Her curtains were open and I could see her walking around her room. She must have been with my son until now.

"Sir?" Barnaby's voice came through.

I had been so engrossed watching Charlotte I had forgotten I was still holding the intercom phone. "Sorry for the trouble, Barnaby," I said. "I thought I needed something, but it turns out I don't."

"That's quite all right, Sir. Goodnight," he said formally.

I wished him goodnight and disconnected the call. Slipping my hands into my pockets I watched her. She had a curvy figure. The kind I liked. Or I used to like. It was so many years ago that I last had even the desire for a woman, I had forgotten how my body felt when I was craving a woman. From this distance she did not look middle aged. She looked to be in her twenties.

I dialed her room number and waited for her to respond.

"Hello?" she said, and I noted the thrill that raced down my flesh.

"Did Zackary just fall asleep?"

"No, he didn't," she said. "I was reading him a story, but somehow I ended up putting the both of us to sleep." The amusement in her tone filtered through and it made me long for a bliss I had never known.

The words left my lips before I could stop them. "I wish I could fall asleep that easily."

"You have trouble falling asleep?"

"Yes," I said slowly. This was not exactly the conversation I wanted to have with one of my staff.

"My mother has insomnia too. It is a remnant from the months before my father passed away."

"I've never been compared to someone's mother before."

"I'm so sorry. I didn't mean in that way. I just meant …"

"Charlotte, relax. It was a bad joke. I'm afraid I'm not used to talking to people anymore."

"Oh," she said, the relief in her voice was obvious.

"What did your father pass away from?"

I could hear her hesitation but she eventually said, "Cancer. It was a long and painful battle."

"My condolences." I could have kicked myself for probing. What was wrong with me? I was behaving like an insensitive prick.

"It's all right. It's been almost seven years now so the pain is no longer as devastating."

"No longer as devastating," I repeated turning the statement over in my mouth. "Is that really true? Does it ever completely heal?"

"No," she replied quietly. "It doesn't. Even when you think it has … it comes back … as fresh as ever, to taunt you with what you lost and can never have back."

We both knew we were no longer talking about her father.

There was an awkward pause. Neither of us knew how to fill it. I heard her take a quick intake of breath.

"You took Zackary out to play today?" I blurted out.

"I did," she said quickly. "We made kites and harassed each other with water balloons. We had a blast, literally." She chuckled to herself.

I found my lips stretching into a smile. It was something that happened often when I was talking to her and hardly at all when I wasn't.

"I have pictures," she said, "but ... how do I send them to you?"

"Do you have a USB stick?"

"Yeah, I think so."

"Save the pictures on it and pass it to Barnaby."

"I'll give it to him in the morning," she said.

"Do you mind if I ... er ... send him to you to tonight?"

"Of course. I'll be awake for at least another hour."

"Thank you. Have a goodnight then, Charlotte."

"Wait ... I mean." She laughed nervously, "I just wanted to say thank you for allowing Zackary to spend time outside. He had a wonderful time today."

"It was your suggestion. It is I who must thank you," I said.

"I'm glad to be able to help," she said softly.

At that moment, all I wanted was to see her face. Know who I was talking to. That was also the moment I knew I had to end the conversation. I was getting too close. "Well, good-night then."

"Brett?" she called, there was a hint of desperation in her voice.

"Yes."

"Do you think … would it be possible for you to make some time to spend with Zackary?"

The idea was like a knife in my heart. She had no idea how much I wanted that. In the tense silence she rushed to explain herself. "It's just that he drew you today. We made a kite and he drew you and his mother. I told him that perhaps the three of you could fly it together someday soon."

"Zackary is terrified of me," I said, my voice sounded harsh with pain.

She did not hesitate. "It didn't seem that way," she said. "In fact, he said … he said that he—" she stopped.

"What did he say?" I asked, and even I could hear how desperately eager I sounded.

"That you smiled a lot. He drew you with a big smile, but he said he had not seen you in a long while."

"Half my face has been gouged out. Did he somehow include that in his drawing?" I asked bitterly.

I heard her draw a sharp breath. "No," she replied. "He drew you with a mask, and painted the smile on top of the mask. You are his father and he loves you."

I think I cried once in my adult life. One night when I didn't want to fight anymore. When the pain was so great and the end seemed so pointless. That one night in a dark pit of despair I thought about ending it all, but it was my love for Zackary that kept me going. Through it all it was him. Hearing her say those words, made a single tear run down my face. I lifted my hand and touched it. Always it was him that could make me cry. "If you can, tell him I love him," I said and cut the connection.

CHAPTER 18

CHARLOTTE

https://www.youtube.com/watch?v=lcOxhH8N3Bo

T ime passed and I stared at the silent intercom. God
knows how long I stood there leaning against
the wall.

My chest seemed eerily clogged as I went over the details of
the call. At first it was to ensure I had not in any way stepped
out of line, but as I ran over his responses again and again,
my cognizance of the words began to fade and I recognized
only the intense and relentless desire to be close to him. To
hold him. Touch him. Comfort him.

I looked out towards his window. It was lighted, but the
curtains were drawn shut. I closed my eyes and tried to
imagine the man in the photo with half his face gouged out,
but I couldn't.

What had given him the impression Zackary was afraid of him?

Especially when Zackary did not behave as if he was. He wouldn't have drawn him, and definitely not with them holding hands. I frowned when I remembered that Zackary did mention his father had made him cry. Were his scars really that awful? Not knowing felt like it would suffocate me. I nearly jumped out of my skin when the knock came on the door.

Shit.

I ran to open the door for Barnaby. He was dressed in the way he always was. Not a hair out of place.

"Just a minute, please," I said and ran back in.

He did not come in, but waited politely outside while I found my spare USB stick and quickly copied the photos onto it.

"There you go," I said, placing it on the little silver plate he held out. It was like a scene from a different century and it made me smile.

"Goodnight, Miss Conrad," he said with a nod. Then he was gone, his footsteps steady and silent, until he was swallowed by the shadows in the corridor.

I closed the door and got ready for bed. Crawling into bed I sought sleep, but it wouldn't come.

"Insomnia …

He said it plagued him. All I usually needed was ten minutes of idleness and my eyelids would become as heavy as wet blankets. But tonight, restless, swirling thoughts kept me wide awake. I punched the pillow and lay on my stomach.

Nope. I turned back and stared at the ceiling. I wondered if he was in bed. I turned on my side and waited for sleep in that position. That didn't work either. I got out of bed and padded over to the window.

His light was still burning.

I sighed and went back to bed. Switching on the bedside lamp I tried to read, but I was too distracted to concentrate. I made my way back to the window. Now I was angry with myself. This was completely stupid and I was behaving like a complete idiot. If my mother knew what I was doing she would be disgusted. God, my father would be turning in his grave if he could see me now.

"He's a married man. Stop lusting after him," I said aloud.

He's married only in name, a voice in my head corrected.

"Well, he's still married."

He's unhappy. Horribly unhappy. She doesn't deserve him.

I slumped on the bed. The craving to go to him was so strong it shocked me. I had never been one to be addicted to anything. I could take or leave chocolate. I tried smoking once and hated it. I went to a club and was given an ecstasy tablet and while I really enjoyed the feeling of being high I never again wanted to have it after I found out that it kills brain cells. But this man was like a drug I had no resistance against. I didn't know why he had such a strong pull over me. It was like he was a giant magnet pulling me to him. I buried my face in my hands.

What the hell have I got myself into?

CHAPTER 19

BRETT

Barnaby was preceded by a quiet knock. He held out his silver plate with the USB stick on it as if it was the most precious thing in the world. He did not know it, but it was. I took it and thanked him. He wished me goodnight and was gone. The first thing I did was bring the stick to my nose. She had held this in her hands. There was no smell. I put it into my laptop and the photos jumped to life on my screen. My hands were shaking as I reached out to touch his face. He was laughing. His clothes were wet and full of dirt and he was laughing!

My son was laughing.

I hadn't seen him laughing in a long time. I enlarged the photo and moved nearer.

"Oh, Zackary, Zackary. My life, my heart. How I love you," I whispered.

I went through the photos. Sometimes I smiled, sometimes I laughed out loud, and then I came across the last one and I froze. Someone else had taken this one. A blonde woman was holding Zackary up in the air, as high as she could. I could see her muscles straining. He was laughing and so was she.

They were both drenched. I could see the shape of her full breasts through her wet clothes. Her nipples were erect from the cold, but that was not what grabbed and refused to let go of my attention.

I stared at her face in amazement.

Charlotte was beautiful. Her blue eyes shone with warmth and intelligence. She was the kind of girl I would have loved to have met before the accident, before I talked myself into marrying Jillian.

CHAPTER 20

CHARLOTTE

The next morning, I walked down from the kitchen with Zackary to find the courtyard brimming with people. Upon inspection I realized that the playground had already been purchased and was being installed.

I was amazed at the speed in which he had acted, even as I tried to ignore the prick in my chest that he hadn't called to inform me of it.

Zackary slipped his hand into mine and tugged to get my attention. "What are they doing?"

"They're building a playground for you," I answered.

His eyes widened. "Like in the park."

I smiled. "Exactly. I think you will love it, and you'll have such a blast playing in there."

"Wow. Is all this just for me?"

I nodded. "You're the luckiest boy in the world, do you know that?" I lowered myself down to his height.

"You have your own personal playground, and a father who loves you so very much. He bought it all, you know? So the next time you see him, you tell him how much you appreciate them, alright?"

He nodded in response and I ruffled his hair. He froze suddenly and jerked away. Taken aback by his response I stared at him as he carefully slicked his hair back.

"But what about Mummy?" he asked.

That was a great question. No doubt Mummy would be very unhappy with this new development that she had no say in. I smiled at Zackary. "I don't see why Mummy won't love it too, can you?" I grinned. "What's not to love? It's swings and slides and sandboxes."

I settled Zackary for breakfast and hurried up to my room. As I approached the intercom, I felt a frisson of anxiety, but I convinced myself that there was no need to be nervous. Perhaps he was no longer even at home. I heard Mrs. Blackmore say that the helicopter had come and taken him to London yesterday.

I pressed the main button, and spoke. "Hello? Brett?"

There was no response.

"Brett," I called again, and already a sensation of longing was settling in the pit of my stomach. I so wanted to hear his voice again. I was just about to disconnect it when his voice came through. My heart jumped to my throat and I could feel my blood rushing in my ear. And this was just the sound of his voice. I had it real bad for this man.

"Charlotte?"

I cleared my throat. "Uh, I just wanted you to know Zackary loves his playground. Thank you for doing that. You make my work so much easier."

"Not at all," he said. "The men will be gone by lunchtime so be sure to create some time for Zackary to use them after his lessons this afternoon."

"I will," I assured. "It will help him loosen up a bit. He is a bit wound up most of the time."

"He is? How so?"

"Um," I hesitated. This was not the reason why I had called and I really didn't want to seem to be complaining or telling tales all the time, but now that I had said it, I had to follow through. "It's not anything serious. After he spends a bit of time with me he'll probably stop being so anal about his hair and clothes and shoes."

He was silent for a while. "I know he will learn to loosen up as time goes on, especially with you in charge of his care. I just want it to happen before he starts school. I don't want him to be different than the other kids or get bullied because he doesn't know how to behave."

"I think he will do very well at school. He is incredibly well mannered."

"I hope so."

"Hey, I wanted to thank you for sending the photos."

"That's okay. He had a really good time."

"I could see that. There was a photo of you too."

I could feel the fire rush up my throat. "Yeah, I wasn't going to send it, but he looked so happy there I thought you might want to see it."

"It was a great photo. I'm glad you sent it. Now I can put a face to your voice."

Something happened between us. The energy changed. We were no longer employer and employee. I swallowed hard. I opened my mouth to answer, but nothing would come out. I don't know whether the heavens took pity on me and saved me, decided to punish me because at that moment, the door to my room burst open and Zackary's mother walked in, an expensive dressing robe tied around her tiny waist.

"What the fuck is going on outside?"

"It's just a little playground for Zackary—"

She folded her arms across her chest, her gaze full of disbelief. "How dare you do something like this without asking my permission?"

"His father—"

"Don't pretend that butter wouldn't melt in your mouth," she snarled. "I know it's you. You instigated this."

I straightened my spine, determined to get a word in edgewise. "Madam—"

But she cut me off again. "I told you to give my son a little time off yesterday in the garden, and you turn his whole life into a circus show?"

"A circus—"

"They praised you as being the best at the agency, however your actions so far have served only to irritate me and make me think you are not the right person for this job." She looked at me as if I disgusted her.

"Could you please let me explain, Madam?"

"No," she said, her voice was cold and hard. "I think you've done enough damage. I've had enough of you trying to undermine me behind my back. You think you can take my place. Hmmm? Well, I've got news for you. You're fired. Pack your things right now and get out of my house. Barnaby will call a taxi for you. Needless to say, I won't be giving you any glowing references."

I felt my own temper rise to the surface. What did this selfish bitch think? That I was desperate for a ride from her? I made my voice cool and uncaring. "I'll be packed and gone in an hour. I don't need a reference from you, glowing or otherwise, and I can get my own taxi."

"We understand each other then. I'll send Mrs. Blackmore to check your luggage before you leave in case you accidentally pack anything that is not yours."

"I wouldn't expect anything less from you. You are classy to the very end."

Her eyes flashed and she was about to say something else when her phone began to ring. When she lifted it up to check the ID, her eyes almost rolled into the back of her head. "Of course," she muttered and with a last glare at me, stormed out of the room.

A barrage of emotions and sensations flooded into me. The first of which was a strange sense of loss which sapped me of all my strength. I had been here less than a week, but it felt like a year. I was just starting to get attached to Zackary ... I had hoped to make a difference and I could already see changes in him. And his father ... I don't know what I wanted or expected from him. It was all getting too complicated. Maybe this was for the best.

I sank on the bed and looked at the wall blankly. It was stupid but my eyes stung with unshed tears. No crying here, Charlotte. You walk out of this place with your head held high. You can cry all you want when you get home, okay. I swallowed the lump in my throat and had just taken a deep calming breath when the intercom crackled.

"Charlotte."

Startled I jumped to my feet. The intercom had been on the whole time. "Brett!"

"Don't do a thing," he said, his voice not warm and friendly but so cold and hard I almost didn't recognize it. "I'll handle this."

The intercom clicked and became silent as he disconnected the line.

CHAPTER 21

BRETT

"Why are you ignoring my calls?" I demanded from the door.

Jillian looked up from her dressing table and regarded me with narrowed eyes. "You came all the way here? I can't wait to hear what can be so important."

I leaned against the door frame and watched her. With a sigh she turned back to her mirror and continued applying her makeup, but her movements were jerky. She was not as calm as she was pretending to be.

"Why did you fire Charlotte?" I asked, walking into her room. Her cloying perfume made specially for her filled my nostrils, reminding me of a time I wanted to forget.

She snorted in disbelief and whirled around on her stool to face me. "She already came running to you? What the hell is going on? Are you fucking her or something?"

"Take your mind out of the gutter. I am not *fucking* her. She is our son's nanny. I was speaking to her on the intercom when you came into her room. What exactly is her offense?"

"When did you become her advocate? And when did it start to matter to you whom I hired or fired?"

"I feel very comfortable having her handle Zackary's care."

"You didn't even want a nanny," she hurled at me.

"That's true, but since you've insisted on one, I now acknowledge that you were right. A nanny is a good idea and I can see Zackary has benefited a lot from Charlotte being here."

She glared at me for a moment and then turned her back on me and gazed at her reflection in the mirror. "She was over stepping her authority, I'll get someone else."

My temper began to rise. "I was the one who bought all the equipment and permitted Zackary to play outside. Come to think of it why would you place all these restrictions on him without informing me about it?"

"When did you suddenly start to care so much about Zackary's welfare? You've left him to me all this while."

"Do you want me to retract that basic right as his mother from you as well? You don't seem very interested in it any longer."

She shot to her feet, her eyes ablaze. "How dare you question my love for my son?"

"Don't test me," I said. "I've allowed you to go whichever way you chose these past years. I won't take such liberties when it comes to Zackary. Either Charlotte stays, or you leave."

Her mouth dropped open. "You would choose a woman who walked into our lives a few days ago over me?"

"Yes."

For a second she stared at me in horror as it became clear to her that I was serious. Then I saw the gears in her brain shift and tears that I had not only no patience for, but found infuriating, began to fill her eyes." Brett, how did we get here? We grew up together. How did I come to mean so little to you? We are a family. She is the outsider. I know what she has been doing. She's been poisoning you against me."

I couldn't believe the words that were coming out of her mouth. Never had I met someone that was as dishonest with herself as she was to everyone else around.

"Jillian, what exactly do I mean to you?"

"I love you, Brett," she cried passionately.

"You sure about that?" I asked as I stripped away my mask.

Her true reaction shone through because she didn't have enough time to hide it. She flinched ... she actually flinched, right before my eyes. Her eyes traced the deep, unbearably ugly scars that lined the right portion of my face. It was a lot better than it had been at the beginning, but the shriveled, disfigured flesh torn from being flung through the window of a somersaulting vehicle then being dragged so hard on gravel that it sandpapered my face right down to the bone in some places, was one she still couldn't stomach.

"Is everything clear now?" I asked, putting the mask back on.

To my surprise, she began to move towards me, lifting her hand up to touch me.

I slapped the hands away before they could connect with my flesh.

"How dare you?"

She winced at the tone of my voice. "You will never forgive me, will you?"

"For what?" I asked and brushed my hair out of my face. "For abandoning me during the hardest time of my life?"

"Brett, I didn't abandon you," she cried. "Aren't I still here? My reaction was normal. Any normal human being would have reacted like that." A sly look came into her eyes. "You think our nanny won't react in exactly the same way if she saw you without your mask?"

My face hardened. Fighting with Jillian was a fool's errand. She was too good at this. I turned away.

"Don't turn away from me please. I'm sorry. I shouldn't have said that. I want to talk about us."

I stopped and turned back. I needed to sort this problem out before I left.

"Anyway, as I was saying, I just needed some time to take it all in ... To readjust ... To see you the way that I used to."

I laughed. "Yes, your method of adjusting was to fuck around. You don't love me, Jillian. You never have. You married me for my money, and I married you because your father asked, you were easy on the eye, and I didn't know then what I do now."

The tears rolled down her eyes. "Brett, your words are too brutal. I'm only human ... and I'm allowed to falter and to disappoint. I'm also allowed to realize my mistakes and change. Why won't you let me in?"

"No one's stopping you," I said. "I'm not. Stop fucking around. Try winning my heart back again ... if you want to."

Her gaze faltered from mine and it almost made me laugh aloud. "What? Too much like work? Or have you finally realized that what you really want is me groveling at your feet for whatever crumbs you want to throw down at me?"

"You still love me, Brett" she said. "That's why you're so bitter."

I shook my head at her arrogance. "Jillian, I'm bitter because I can't believe that I once deluded myself into marrying you. I'm even more bitter now because I can't get rid of you as easily as I would like to. I have a responsibility to Zackary and unlike you I take the magnitude of what that entails seriously."

"It doesn't matter what you think, I *am* a good mother to Zackary."

"Whatever. I've got to go, but leave Charlotte alone, or I'll take matters into my own hands and I assure you, you won't like it."

I turned around and walked out of her room.

At the top of the stairs, I froze. Heading towards me from the servants' stairs was Charlotte, her eyes were on the floor. She must have been heading to the kitchen. Before she could raise her head to notice me, Jillian's words came to taunt me. *You think our nanny won't react in exactly the same way if she saw you without your mask?* I experienced an instinctive desire to turn around and go the opposite way, to hide from her.

But she raised her head and saw me.

We walked towards each other. She was staring at me, her blue eyes wide. Both of us had slowed down our pace, but we did not stop as we moved nearer and as we passed each other I could feel my heart hammering in my chest. Hell, she was even more beautiful in real life.

God, I wanted her.

"Brett," she called.

I didn't respond. I didn't want to keep going, I didn't want to ignore her. I wanted her to speak … and I wanted to look properly at her … and into her eyes, but I couldn't bring myself to stop walking.

"Brett," she called louder, and this time my feet came to a halt of their own accord. I didn't turn around. I could feel the rush of adrenaline in my veins as the sound of her shoes turning to come to me hit my ears. My command was automatic.

"Stay where you are."

She obeyed.

"What is it?" I asked.

Silence.

Slowly, I turned around to face her.

CHAPTER 22

CHARLOTTE

My mouth was open, but I simply could not make it work.

Brett was standing in front of me! There was a mask over his face made of some kind of shiny material, probably not material, but silicone. It was dark, a sharp contrast to the pale ivory of his skin. It was obvious he had not been out in the sun in years. His hair was swept away from his face in waves, and just underneath his right eye, I could see a glimpse of the mangled damaged flesh as it rode down and disappeared underneath the mask.

Jillian had inferred that he was hideous … a monster… but he was not. The man I had seen in the picture paled in comparison. From the broadened shoulders upon which a striped, white dress shirt was draped to the charcoal slacks tailored to run down his long muscular legs, there was no doubt I was staring at the sexiest, most magnetic man I'd ever seen. Maybe it was his hooded eyes, or lightly tousled hair, or the mystery the mask exuded, but to my mind he was as dark and mysterious as a romantic hero in a novel.

My hand came to my chest in confusion. I wanted to say something, something that would let him know that I did not find him repulsive, quite the contrary in fact, but not a word could I bring to my lips. I could feel my face become redder as the seconds passed.

"Charlotte," he called.

I looked at him dumbly. Inside I was screaming abuse at myself. *Say something, idiot. Say something. Anything.*

"Will you go and see my wife? She has something to say to you."

I nodded and hurried away like a little coward. Still cursing myself I found my way over to Jillian's suite. When I arrived, went in without even knocking, my brain was so scrambled.

She was standing by the window and gazing out. Her blonde hair was arranged at the nape of her neck in a beautiful bun, but she was still in her dressing gown. For a moment I was struck by the sight. There was something so sad and lost about her. She turned at my entrance, her eyes widened with hope. She must have thought I was Brett, because her face changed to great dislike, maybe even hate, when she saw me.

"What do you want?" she spat.

"Mr. King said you wanted to see me."

Her hands clenched at her sides and she took a deep breath.

"Well, if it was nothing, I'll go pack my things."

She exhaled loudly. "No need," she said through gritted teeth. "You'll be staying ... for now. Zackary's father wanted me to give you a second chance but, be forewarned, one mistake on your part and you are out of here." She walked to her dressing table, sat down on the stool and started to touch up her already perfectly made up face.

I was dismissed, but such emotions raced through me I couldn't move. I felt almost dizzy. Brett had forced her to let me remain … what did that mean?

"Why are you still here?" she asked.

It instantly brought me right back to earth. I took a backward step, then another. Then I turned around, exited the room, and all but crept down the corridor. My heart felt as if it was a bird trapped in my chest and it was flapping its little wings like crazy. All my nervous energy was for nothing. Brett was no longer at the spot we met before. Even so, the mere fact of thinking he might have been there gave me a headache. I headed to my room and sat on the bed. I needed to clear my head.

The intercom began to bleep. I could see that it was from the kitchen. I quickly answered it. It was Mrs. Blackmore.

"Zackary's almost done with his meal, where are you?" she asked, a hint of impatience in her voice. "His tutor will be here soon."

"I'm on my way," I said, and bolted out of my room.

When I arrived at the kitchen, Zackary was sitting at the table and idly kicking his heels against the chair's legs. There was a tray of breakfast on a table.

"Who's that for?" I asked.

Mrs. Blackmore looked up from her phone, her gaze nervous, and her feet tapping rapidly against the stone floor. "It's for Mr. King. He's supposed to be leaving soon and for the love of God I cannot find Steven or Carrie to take it up to him."

I spoke before I could use my brain. "Why don't I take it over?"

She turned to me. It took a few moments for her to process the logistics of such an action through her mind, and I spent that time wondering what the hell was wrong with me. I just met him in the corridor and acted like a complete nutcase, and now I was offering to take his breakfast up to him.

"Yes, that's a good idea," she said in a relieved voice. "Just leave it on the table by the door. Do not go into his rooms … or linger. And come straight back."

"Okay."

She picked up the tray and thrust it at me. "Quickly now. I'll keep the lad here until you return."

I took the tray from her and had reached the top of the stairs when I realized I wasn't sure which corridor to take. I was standing there, trying to work out my East from my West when I saw Melly.

"Mr. King's suite? Keep going straight down." She nodded towards the corridor behind me. "It's the first door on your left, you can't miss it. The hallway has a gallery of portraits."

"Thanks, Melly."

"Hey, want to go out for a drink, Friday?"

My stomach was churning with nervousness, but I smiled and nodded. "Sure, why not."

"Great. See you later," she said, and I turned to go towards Mr. King's rooms.

I followed her instructions and pretty soon I was standing in front of an imposing mahogany door. I knocked, twice, and when there was no response, pulled down the handle, and pushed it open.

Gentle morning light was pouring in from a walk-in balcony straight ahead, but I also noted the presence of candlelight deeper in the rooms. The stone walls were very bare, the furniture sparse and simple. There was something hermit-like and yet there was a clandestine ambience about the suite. As Mrs. Blackmore had indicated there was a table by the door.

I should have put the tray there and left, but I didn't.

CHAPTER 23

A s if guided by a secret instinct and a destiny I had no control over, I took a step into the room. My hands were gripping the tray so hard, my knuckles were white. I turned and headed towards the left where the candles flickered and danced.

I passed the first room which was a bedroom with a very big wooden bed. The sheets were crumpled. My progress was silent since I was almost tip-toeing. As I moved halfway into the room I could look into the adjoining room. It was a dressing room. I could see an oval mirror.

I heard a noise coming from there and froze. As I stood there unmoving, terrified, and yet unable to stop myself, he appeared. He was walking across the room to the other side. Without his shirt, he seemed even larger, his torso tight with well-defined muscles, but even more astonishingly, he was not wearing his mask!

My eyes were riveted to his disfigured face. Oh, God! It was incredible. I never imagined it would be so bad. I could not stop staring at the mangled flesh, the raised white scars, the skin stretched so tightly over his cheekbone it looked painful. As I gaped in astonishment, he walked past the mirror.

For just a few seconds, I saw the other side of him reflected in the mirror. The unscarred side.

That man was beautiful beyond anything I had known. The man I had seen in the photo was young. He had taken from life what he wanted. He was at the peak of his achievement and tasted success. He had never known loss or horror, and he looked out to the world with some arrogance. But this man … this man had known terrible, terrible pain and hurt. He had been to the pits of despair, maybe even given up on life, and then forced himself to carry on. His suffering was stamped on the fine lines around his eyes and mouth, on his skin, in his gorgeous eyes.

I felt my heart soar as if it would fly out of my body. Wow! That was the moment I fell in love with the man in the mirror.

When he had passed out of my sight, I turned around and quickly went back out to the room filled with morning light. I placed the tray on top of the polished surface of the table, taking care not to make a sound, and then straightened to take my leave. The sound of his voice reached me before I could get to the door.

"Running away, Charlotte?"

I stopped in my tracks. I knew he had not seen me. He could not have. "No," I replied glancing back. He had his mask back on his face and he had pulled on a shirt. It hung unbuttoned on his body. I could see his abs, hard and strong and I guessed that must be how he passed his hours of solitude, working out on his own.

"Do you know how to knot a tie?" He held out a blood-red tie up to me and I went towards it like a lamb to slaughter.

I took the tie from him, careful to avoid skin contact. He walked away from me. He said something else before it struck me that he was on the phone and speaking in another language. He turned to head towards his desk as he spoke, his voice low and rapid as he flipped a file open and began to peruse it.

I stood in the middle of the room, trying to keep my attention solely focused on fashioning the tie into a decent knot, but my hands were trembling so much I was making a mess of it. I sensed his conversation was dwindling down and I clumsily tried to undo it and start again.

He finished his call and the room felt silent until I felt him approaching me. "You don't know how to do it?"

"I'm afraid it's not very good."

"Don't nannies have to learn to dress their charges?" he asked softly.

"Yes, but not while their hearts are racing." I turned to face him.

"Is your heart racing?" The almost translucent gray of his irises bore into mine.

My heart responded by thumping so hard against my chest I was sure he could hear it. Close up, his nearness was almost unbearable. I wanted to rip the mask off and show him that I didn't care about his scars and his mangled flesh.

I wanted to press my body against his and feel his mouth on mine.

The air between us changed, became thick and viscous. I felt as if I needed to breathe and couldn't. There was so much I wanted to say. So much I couldn't say.

"Thanks for bringing my breakfast," he murmured, never taking his eyes off me.

"You're ... uh ... welcome. And I ... um ... I wanted to thank you for helping me with Mrs. King earlier today."

"No need," he replied, his lips twisted. "I know you'll do a good job."

I really wanted to stay with him in that room full of shadows, and full of the clean smell of his aftershave, to say all the things I wanted to say to him, to touch his skin and tell him he was beautiful, but I knew I couldn't. This was the end of the road for me. At least, for now. I came to bring the breakfast and that was done. Mrs. Blackmore was probably having kittens by now. I placed the poorly knotted tie on the table. "I guess, I should go. Zackary is waiting for me."

He didn't say anything, just watched me with those extraordinary eyes. I wondered if he watched me as I left. I wanted him to.

CHAPTER 24

BRETT

I wanted Charlotte. Fuck, how I wanted her. While I drowned in those baby blue eyes, the smell of her skin wrapped itself around me, making me crave her taste. It was inappropriate and I felt like a pervert, but damnit I couldn't help myself.

I wanted my son's nanny.

Her beauty was not obvious like Jillian's, but was the kind that you grew into. The longer you looked the more you found to admire, and if you allowed it, it led you into deep addiction. That was how exquisite she was.

It began from her voice; the best way I could describe it was mesmerizing. When she spoke it seized you in the gut. You never wanted her to stop. Then there was her body. It was all woman, from her full breasts to those curvy legs it all screamed feast. It was enough to stop any man cold. I watched her hips, in dark jeans, sway gently as though to a tune only she could hear as she left my quarters.

I had a raging hard on. Until she had come I had not even

thought of having a woman. Now all I wanted to do was bury my face between her legs, and make her threaten to tear the hair off my scalp as I ravaged her cunt.

Jesus Christ. I couldn't even sleep at night anymore because I kept thinking of her. I woke up hard and jerked off thinking of her breasts in my hands. Kneading, sucking, nipping. I imagined her begging for my hard cock. I rammed so deep inside her she screamed. In my fantasy, I felt the heat of her tight pussy milking my dick while I fucked her and heard the helpless cries and whimpers ringing around me.

Oh, how I fucked her.

I came in a rush of hot semen. There was so much of it. I closed my eyes, and even then, I thought of her body trembling gently under me ... the heat of her sweet breath on my face.

With her I knew I would be able to feel again. Being with her would go beyond just sexual ecstasy, and bring to me the warmth that I craved no matter how brief. It had been so long since I felt anything. For a long time I thought I would never smile again and yet with effortless ease she made me laugh. I didn't want my darkness to rub off on her, but who could blame me if I wanted a taste of the light that I knew came with Charlotte?

I also knew she was not one to be tasted, then let go. One taste and I would be hooked, but keeping her was not in the cards. My situation was already complicated enough. After what happened this morning, it was obvious Jillian hated her and was probably planning on how to get rid of her. Any sign of interest from me would be the final nail in the coffin. Charlotte was good for Zackary and there was no way I was going to put myself before my son's needs. I had been selfish my whole life. This time I was going to put Zackary first.

No matter how difficult it was, I planned to keep my distance. For her sake, and for Zackary's too. I think I did quite well the whole day. I kept up a tough schedule and only returned after dinner. I planned on going to see Zackary later. For too long that was my only pleasure. Stealing into his room in the dead of night and simply watching him sleep. Since Charlotte arrived I had not seen him and I longed to.

As I walked into my rooms I found myself glancing at the intercom on the wall. So quickly it had become a habit I especially looked forward to. The conversations were harmless, or so I wanted to believe. I would get to know about Zackary's progress, and briefly hear her voice. I rang her extension.

"Hello, Brett," she whispered.

I felt myself melt. "Hello, Charlotte." I paused. Make this about Zackary. "How was Zackary's day?"

"Good. We had a good day. He got to try out his new playground. He fell once and scraped his knee, but he was very brave about it. He didn't cry or complain."

I felt my heart swell with pride. I always wanted him to be brave. "That's good."

"I … uh … I was … uh … wondering if … well, if Zackary could perhaps have dinner with you tomorrow? It's just that he ate alone today and he looked really pitiful."

I was too stunned to respond.

She went on. "I believe your wife will not be home tomorrow night so I thought that perhaps it would be a good opport—"

Anger coiled in the pit of my stomach. "Do you think that I purposefully choose not to spend any time with my son?"

I thought that she would cower then, especially at the bite of my tone, but she pressed undaunted. "You said that he is scared of you. I know he's not, but even if he was, maybe if you made a little bit more effort to—"

I disconnected the call and stood there staring at the intercom. How dare she insinuate I wasn't trying hard enough? I tried and tried, but after the accident, anytime I came within sight of my son he would break out in silent tears. And if I insisted on approaching, he would explode into hysterics of fright and horror.

His reaction tore at my heart, but he was only a child and he didn't understand that just because I looked like a monster I was not one. I left him alone after Jillian got worried that he would become unnecessarily fearful or even develop psychological problems. "As he gets older," she assured me, "he will come to understand. Just be patient."

I ached to spend time with him, but I knew she was right. He needed time. The days grew into weeks, and the months into years, and until Charlotte came I honestly thought he had all but forgotten me.

It was not Charlotte's fault. She was only trying to help. I shouldn't have taken my pain out on her. I wanted to call her back to apologize for being so harsh, but I decided against it. Maybe it was better this way. She had too much power over me already. Boundaries between us was a good thing.

CHAPTER 25

CHARLOTTE

I wanted to call him back, but I stepped away and reminded myself of the fact that seemed to be slipping my mind more often than it should have.

He was my employer!

I spent the rest of the night waiting for him to call me back. April called and I found it almost impossible to tell her how I felt. We had always shared everything, but I couldn't share this with her yet. Not yet. I just needed a bit of time to savor it for myself. I knew I was in love with him, but I didn't allow myself to think of the consequences.

At least not yet.

If I told April she would tell me in no uncertain terms the consequences, which of course, I knew, but was pretending not to for a little while longer. A man like that I was sure would leave you clawing holes into sheets, but he would also leave your heart smashed and splattered on the cold floor.

Before I fell asleep I began to understand that I had truly offended him earlier. I couldn't understand why he would not even try to spend a little time with Zackary. It was not like I was asking him to take his mask off. The boy was indeed a child, but old enough to appreciate that his father wore a mask.

A little coaxing on his part would have been more than enough to get rid of his fear towards his father. In fact, even the fear was hard to comprehend as his father looked anything but monstrous. Despite the mask, he was a man that would walk into a room and command the attention of all.

This was the first cold evening since my arrival here so I pulled the covers up to my chin and tried to will myself to sleep despite the tug of arousal in the pit of my belly. I was just about to fall asleep when I heard the screams.

I jerked my body upright. The cries were coming from the baby monitor. Zackary! In an instant I had shot out of bed, run across my room, and threw open the connecting door.

He was sitting up in the bed howling like an animal in pain. I ran up to him and pulled him into my arms but he wouldn't stop wailing.

"What's the matter?" I asked, trying to figure out what was wrong but he wouldn't stop ... Not even to speak.

I threw on his bedside lamp and quickly inspected his body. There were no injuries. What was going on?

"Mummy!" he kept calling out. "Mummy! Don't die, Mummy," he wailed. His pitiful cries tore at my heart.

"Zackary," I called but he wouldn't respond. "Your mother

has gone to London. She'll be back tomorrow," I lied. I knew she wasn't back tomorrow.

I held him and rocked him, but he was becoming more and more distressed. I never thought I would say it, but I wished more than ever that his mother was around or even his dad. The door to the room opened then and I looked up in despair, expectant, only to see that it was Mrs. Blackmore.

"What's going on?" she asked as she adjusted her robe. "I could hear him crying all the way from my room."

"I think it was a nightmare."

"Please don't die, Mummy," he screamed again.

Mrs. Blackmore frowned. "You can't calm him down?"

I shook my head.

She reached out to wipe the tears away from his face. "Oh dear. This could go on a while."

"Does he usually have nightmares like this?"

"Sometimes, usually when his mother is away."

I looked down at him, the croak in his voice too painful to listen to. "Come on, darling. Everything is fine. Mummy is fine. Do you want to call her on the telephone?"

"Mummy!" he wailed.

"I don't think that's a good idea," Mrs. Blackmore muttered, shaking her head vehemently.

I rocked him gently. "He keeps calling for his mother though …"

"No, no, she doesn't want to be disturbed unless it is a real emergency. That means blood or fire."

"What if we get his father?" I suggested.

She nodded. "Maybe that will help. I'll wait here. You go and get him."

"Me?"

"Go on. Hurry up. The sooner we sort this out the sooner everyone can get to bed." She moved forward briskly and took the boy from me.

I got up. "All right."

I ran from the room and headed over to his wing. At first I had been driven by desperation to help Zackary, but as I approached, the doubt set in. *I had already upset him earlier. Wasn't I pushing it?*

I thought hard. Would this make him come with me? Mrs. King had instructed me during my interview to call on his father should there be any emergency, but Mrs. Blackmore had already dismissed this as unworthy to be classed as an emergency. Beyond the fact that I thought of this as an opportunity for Zackary to hold the boy there was nothing.

But that didn't stop me.

I lifted my hand and knocked on his door. Even if it got me fired it would still be worth it.

There was no response.

I knocked again and still there was no response. So I boldly opened the door and walked into the suite of rooms. The lounge was dark, the only lighting from the courtyard below, and the moonlight filtering in from above.

CHAPTER 26

CHARLOTTE

"Mr. King?" I called. "Mr. King?"

His bedroom door was open, but there even I dared not go. I stood a foot away from it. "Mr. King," I called, this time around, louder and more determined and his response came.

"Charlotte?"

"Yes, it's me."

He appeared at the door then. The sculpt of his broad, bare shoulders loomed like a dark silhouette that slimmed down to his hips. Every time I was near him I was once again conscious of his imposing height. I realized he was unmasked. Even though it was too dark to make out his features, I could sense the incredible tension in his body. Like a big cat ready to spring.

"What's wrong?" he growled.

"Zackary," I began to say, but as usual, my brain fried in his presence.

"What is it?" he repeated urgently.

I brought myself back to reason. "Zackary had a nightmare. Mrs. Blackmore and I can't calm him down."

He stood very still saying nothing.

"He needs you."

"Have you contacted his mother?"

"Mrs. King said I shouldn't unless it was a real emergency. She advised me to contact you instead."

"I can't come," he said, and I heard the pain in his voice. "He'll calm down."

My heart fell at his words, but I wasn't giving up. "He's calling out for his … a parent. Neither Mrs. Blackmore nor I can answer to that."

He turned his back to me. "Leave," he ordered, closing the door in my face.

I looked around in frustration, the sight of Zackary's drenched face and snot-clogged nose emboldened me. I went forward and pushed the door open.

"You might fire me for this," I said. "But I don't care. Your little boy needs *you*. Right now, it is not a role that a nanny or a housekeeper can fill in for. If you love him as much as I think you do you'll go down and make it better for him."

"Charlotte, get off my back," he growled, but I wasn't fazed. I fisted my hands and held my ground. We glared at each other in the dim light, and then he shut his eyes to control his temper.

"What do you want me to do, Sir?" I asked, deliberately using the formal term of address.

"He'll calm down."

"Of course he will, eventually … but it would be truly helpful if one of his parents could talk to him. Ask him why he is so damn terrified and listen to him …" I paused. "Or he'll grow up emotionally derelict."

"He'll survive," he said harshly. "I basically grew up the same way."

"Are you perfectly happy with who you are?" I asked. "If you are then I'll leave."

He came towards me, and without conscious effort my leg took a step backwards. He stopped in front of me. "Why are you backing away?"

"I don't know," I said, and truer words had never been spoken.

Again, he took a step forward and I took one backwards. At this point I was sure that he was just testing me.

He stopped, and so did I.

"Answer my question … Sir," I said to him, "and I promise I will leave and never ask you to talk or spend time with your son again."

My chest was heaving at this point, my breathing fast and loud. I could feel the goose pimples as they erupted and ran down my skin. I was scared but I was excited too. I had pulled the tiger's tail. I didn't know what the tiger would do. The tension in the air was thick enough to cut through.

Suddenly he moved. So fast I didn't know what hit me. I yelped as my back slammed into the wall. Then he was against me, his eyes boring into mine. His heat filled my senses and his breath was hot against my forehead. In the illumination of the moon his eyes glittered and I could almost trace out his scars. We were only inches away from a light switch. If I hit it he would see that I didn't care about his scars. My hand started moving upwards. His hand closed around my wrist. My eyes slid up to his eyes, then down to his lips.

"Brett …" I did not recognize my own voice. It was so hoarse. It was also an invitation. I wanted him to kiss me.

"What do you think, little Miss Know It All?" he asked me. "Do I seem perfectly happy with the way I am?"

Every part of me was frozen. I couldn't move, much less speak.

"Nothing to say?" he taunted.

"I want to leave," I finally managed to croak out.

"Zackary reacting as though I truly am a monster hurts me more than you could possibly imagine," he said quietly.

I stiffened with shock. How insensitive I have been.

"Try your best to quiet him down. I'll call his mother and get her to come to him." He released my hand and walked away. The cold air that replaced his warmth was like a slap. I started shivering. It took a few moments for me to stabilize myself before I fled from his room. I returned to Zackary to meet him in Mrs. Blackmore's arms, still sobbing quietly. He lifted his head the moment he heard me and kept his gaze on me as I came to sit on the bed.

"Zackary," I called and he sat up from Mrs. Blackmore's hold, wiping his red and swollen eyes. It was heartbreaking.

"Why are you crying?" I asked.

"Mummy," he sobbed. "I think she's dead."

My heart skipped a beat, and I shared a look with Mrs. Blackmore.

"What do you mean?" she asked him.

He tried to get his words out between spurts of crying and sniffing. He was truly just a baby and my heart went out to him. "She had … an accident … I saw it … her car … it went over and over and over and she died."

"It was just a nightmare, sweetheart. Your mother is fine," I cajoled. To my surprise, he spread his arms out and flew into my arms. I held him to me, wanting to help, and not knowing how to.

"What happened with Mr. King?" Mrs. Blackmore asked curiously.

"He said he would get in contact with Madam and see if she can come back."

Her eyes widened in surprise. "That's not going to go down too well."

I hugged Zackary closer to me. My heart was weeping for him. I had grown up with both my parents utterly devoted to me and I couldn't even begin to understand what his life must be like with a psychotic mother and a father he never saw.

I could tell Mrs. Blackmore wanted to ask more, but out of

concern for the little boy still clinging to my arms, she held in her curiosity. Patting his hair affectionately she cooed words of comfort. Soon he quieted down and started to fall asleep in my arms. Mrs. Blackmore took her leave and I settled Zackary down to sleep. I stayed until I was sure he was asleep. Mrs. King never called.

I was actually angry with her. What would it have taken for her to call and tell the boy she was fine? Nothing. Yet, she had not done it. Her fun was more important. I switched off his main light and leaving the connecting door open, I went back to my room. Just as I was settling into bed the intercom began to beep. I knew who it was. I went up to answer it.

I shut my eyes at the barrage of feelings that hit me. This was the man I was in love with. My employer. A married man. A man so scarred he had to wear a mask in public. A man wounded. A man I could not have. And yet I had the memory of how close he was to me. His eyes staring into mine. The warmth of his body encapsulating me …

"Yes," I answered, my voice was barely above a whisper.

"How is he?"

"Better," I replied. "He has fallen asleep."

"Did you find out why he was so upset?"

"He had a nightmare that his mother was in an accident. It scared him. I wanted him to speak to her. Were you not able to get in touch with her?"

"No," came his response. "I tried, but her phone is switched off."

"Hmm … Never mind. It's fine."

"Perhaps. Goodnight, Charlotte."

I thought about apologizing for my intrusion earlier. "I'm really sorry about bursting into your room. I don't normally do things like that. I was just very worried about Zackary."

"Thank you for caring, Charlotte. It is a rare and extremely precious quality."

Then he ended the call.

CHAPTER 27

CHARLOTTE

I'd tossed and turned all night unable to find sleep and when I eventually did, I was awake by dawn. I tip-toed into Zackary's room and found him sleeping soundly. Not wanting to disturb him, I used the servants' stairs where I wouldn't be seen by anybody and slipped into the kitchen. Mrs. Blackmore was already up and working the mix for her famous American style thick pancakes.

At the sight of my groggy eyes, she laughed and went to the coffee maker. A cup of steaming coffee was put in front of me. I showered her with a smile of gratitude.

"Hard night for us all," she said as I took a sip of the divine liquid. "The police brought Mrs. King home."

My eyes popped open. "What?" I cried.

"All I know is Carrie said she heard them arrive at about 4.00 a.m. Mr. Boothworth met them outside," she said. "I'm waiting on him to come in for breakfast and give us the lowdown."

Before I could say anything Mr. Boothsworth arrived impeccably dressed in his official uniform.

"I'll have a batch of those, Mrs. Blackmore," he said, "but with yoghurt instead of chocolate."

Mrs. Blackmore looked like she was about to refuse, but must have remembered the information she was about to extract, so nodded in agreement. "Of course, Mr. Boothsworth." She smiled broadly. "What happened last night? I heard that even Mr. King came down to attend to the police."

Glancing at my steaming mug of coffee, he decided to extract one more request. "A cup of Earl Grey would be a dream this morning," he said at no one.

I had to drop my face to my cup to hide my amusement. They were such a pair. It was a shame they were not together.

With a blank face, Mrs. Blackmore made him a cup and plopped it hard enough before him to make a little liquid slop out of the side. His response was to jerk away exaggeratedly as if he was saving himself from burns. Again, it made me suspect that Melly was right. Something had happened between them and it was unresolved and itching to be scratched.

Calmly, he took a sip from his drink before making his announcement. "Mrs. King was involved in an accident in the wee hours of this morning."

The humorous situation dissipated instantly. Both Mrs. Blackmore and I froze.

Mr. Boothsworth put his cup down. "Fortunately, she came

out rather almost unscathed, but her ... um," he cleared his throat, "male companion was knocked unconscious when the vehicle rammed into a street pole. They rushed him to the hospital. It doesn't seem too severe. At least I hope it isn't."

"How is Madam now?" Mrs. Blackmore asked worriedly.

"Needed a stitch on her forehead, which she has just been hysterical about, but no doubt, it'll pass."

"How weird because Zackary had a nightmare during the night," Mrs. Blackmore said. "He dreamt his mother was in an accident and wouldn't stop crying. We even had to ask Mr. King to come over."

Mr. Boothsworth stopped sipping from his cup and turned to the both of us, his eyes wide and suspicious, as if he suspected us of trying to trick him. For a brief moment, he bore a striking resemblance to Lurch from the Addams family, and although there was nothing funny about what had happened, I had to bite back a smile.

"How could the child know?" he asked bewildered. He leaned towards me. "Does he have some sort of—"

"Don't talk such nonsense," Mrs. Blackmore instantly shut him down.

"Why?" he retorted. "I'd like to know how the boy knew."

"Most children have better intuition than adults do," I said, the explanation sounded silly, but it was definitely a very odd coincidence.

Mr. Blackmore was scornful. "That doesn't explain anything."

The door to the kitchen swung open then and in came Bella,

one of the maids. She was dressed in the white apron and striped green uniform of the mansion.

"It seems to be an early morning for everyone," Mrs. Blackmore noted to the brunette.

She had come to deliver messages from Mrs. King. She addressed me first. "Mrs. King ... wants you to take Zackary to her as soon as you can."

"Sure. I'll go wake him up," I said, finishing my coffee.

She turned to Mrs. Blackmore. "Also, she wants her usual breakfast of dry toast with a scraping of butter, and a cup of tea, Mrs. Blackmore. Please hurry up, because she is like a bear with a sore head this morning."

I took the old wooden stairs two at a time. I guess I was eager to see the relations between mother and child. Part of me still couldn't quite believe how Zackary could have known his mother was in danger the previous evening, but the fact it happened was pretty amazing. Anyway, as much as I disliked her I was glad for Zackary's sake she had returned unscathed. It would have otherwise been a very different atmosphere in the castle and the poor child didn't need another problem on his little plate.

I quickly woke him up and told him his mother wanted to see him. He hopped out of bed in his eagerness to be with her. I stood back and watched him comb his hair carefully, then we set off for his mother's wing. I knocked softly on her door and smiled encouragingly at him. When she bade us enter I pushed open the door.

She was lying in bed in a pretty nightgown with a matching gown. There was a plaster on her left forehead very close to her hairline, and another on her elbow, but otherwise she looked as fit as a fiddle.

"Oh, darling," she cried, opening her pale arms. "Come to Mummy. I heard you had an awful nightmare last night, you poor little thing."

The boy ran up to her, scrambled on the bed, and settled happily against her body. They were exactly the same shade of blonde. With him enclosed in her arms she turned her hostile eyes up to me. "You may leave now. Come and pick him up in about half an hour."

I was actually going to say something nice to her, but I realized she hated me and nothing I was going to do, or say was going to change that. Anyway, she wasn't my favorite person either.

"Okay, I'll be back in half an hour," I said, and walked out of her bedroom. I took a couple of steps away from her door, but then, something made me stop. I knew I could get caught, but I couldn't stop myself. I had to know. There was something very wrong about the situation in this household, I was pretty certain it was being deliberately fostered. I went back to her door and put my ear against the keyhole.

"I was so scared, sweetheart. It was horrible. Just horrible. I mean I could have died last night," she was saying.

"No, Mummy," Zackary gasped.

"I'm afraid so, darling. You almost became an orphan last night."

Zackary began to cry softly. "I don't want you to die, Mummy."

"Well, I was lucky this time. An angel sat on my shoulder and protected me, because little Zackary needs a Mummy."

"What's that then?"

"Oh that. It was just a little stitch."

"Will you have ugly scars like Daddy?" he asked.

"Don't worry, I won't turn into an ugly monster like Daddy. I love you and I'll never stop loving you no matter what."

"How do you know Daddy doesn't love us?"

"For instance: weren't you scared last night when you thought I almost died?"

I heard a sniff and I assumed he nodded because she carried on. "Don't cry again my dear. You were happy to see me because you care for me, but daddy didn't even bother to ask me how I felt, or how I was doing. Isn't that terribly mean of him?"

There was no response. "Why doesn't Daddy love us?"

"He used to," she said, "but that's the thing about accidents, they change people. It made not only his face but also his heart ugly. It's not his fault, he can't help the way he is, but that is why I can never trust him to be alone with you. You won't ever stay in the same room as Daddy, will you?"

"What about if Charlotte is in the room?" Zackary asked.

At that moment I heard footsteps in the corridor and I quickly straightened and walked away. It was Melly, balancing some bags of shopping and a thick file.

"You still on for tonight, right?" she asked.

"Definitely," I said, smiling broadly, even though my heart was thumping in my chest. If what I had heard was an example of how Mrs. King interacted with the boy in private then, it was no wonder at all that the boy was not only terrified of his father, but also paranoid about her. In one short conversation she had managed to poison the child against his father and make it appear as if she could die at any moment and he could lose her forever.

CHAPTER 28

E xactly half an hour later, I knocked on Mrs. King's door. When she called enter, I pushed it open, and announced, "I'm here, Madam."

She lifted her head to gaze at me. "I will be heading to Winslow to see my Aunt today. I need to rest and since I want to spend more time with Zackary there will be no need to come along. Cancel his swimming lessons at ... what time is it?"

"2:30pm," I replied.

"Right. Cancel that, and get luggage packed with his things, enough for a few days."

"Yes, Madam."

"When are you meant to have your day off?"

"On Sunday," I replied.

"Today is ...?"

"Thursday."

"Doesn't matter. Just take the time off until I return."

"Alright," I responded. "Thank you."

"Get his breakfast ready, then come back for him."

I could have taken the child with me then, but she wanted to treat me like a lowly servant. Gritting my teeth I smiled at Zackary. Then I headed down the stairs determined I wouldn't let her get to me, but there was no fooling Mrs. Blackmore.

"What's wrong?" she asked, her brows furrowed with concern.

"Nothing a good breakfast won't cure. What is Zackary having today?" I asked her.

"Oatmeal."

"I guess you can start to prepare it. I'm supposed to bring him down for breakfast now."

"Why didn't you just bring him down with you?"

"Madam wanted a few more minutes with him," I said with a tight smile.

"Charlotte, you don't look so well," Carrie noted, looking up from her cup of coffee.

"Mr. Boothsworth, how scared is Zackary of his father?"

Mrs. Blackmore answered for him. "Carrie told me George, the last chauffeur, told her how Mr. King had waited by his door for Zackary to come back from a trip to his Aunt's, but when Zackary saw him he ran back out to the car and shut the door. George told her he was trembling."

"That was nothing," Mr. Boothsworth said, his tone doleful. "On his second birthday Mr. King threw him a party. He didn't participate in the event but came at the end of it to give the boy a present. The moment Mr. King appeared Zackary started crying and looking at his mother for reassurance."

"I know he's a kid, but really someone should sit him down and be firm with him. I wouldn't let my son treat me like that. It's the strangest thing. He should have been used to it by now. It's very strange because children that age are usually so good about accepting their parents exactly as they are."

I had a good idea where his hysterics could have originated from, but I didn't say. "How did the accident happen?" I asked Mr. Boothsworth. "You were around at the time, weren't you?"

"This one's been around a long while," Mrs. Blackmore said sarcastically.

"I'm capable of commitments," he insinuated, and for a moment I was pushed out of the conversation.

She gave him a sour look before returning to the batch of flapjacks she was pulling out of the oven.

He turned to me. "It was three years ago," he said. "Mr. Stanley Wilde, Madam's father was in the car with Mr. King. They were on their way from the airport when the driver of a truck carrying flammable liquid fell asleep at the steering wheel. His truck rammed into them. The impact flung their car off the road and into the woods. The leaking tank blew the entire vehicle up. Luckily Mr. King was flung out since he wasn't wearing a seat belt, but Mr. Wilde wasn't so lucky. Mr. Wilde was like a father to him in many ways and I think it was a devastating blow to him. He was driving, you see. After the accident, he completely shut off."

"What was Mr. King like before the accident? More approachable?"

"Oh, no. He's always been guarded. The only person he truly opened up to was the Madam's father and of course, he fell in love with Zackary from the day he was born."

"Do you think he tolerates all her affairs because he feels guilty?" Mrs. Blackmore asked.

For a moment the butler stopped and looked between us, then he rose to his feet, a look of dignity on his face. "Being with you women for even a few minutes has turned me into a tattler."

"You don't need us. You've always been one," Mrs. Blackmore growled.

"I'll take my flapjacks to go," he said and rose to finish off his tea elsewhere.

Mrs. Blackmore finished putting Zackary's breakfast together and I rose too. It was time for me to go get him.

CHAPTER 29

CHARLOTTE

I dressed in a pair of slim fitting blue jeans and a pretty pink sweater for my night out with Melly. Then, sitting on my bed, I Facetimed April.

"Whoa! You look amazing. What happened to the sackcloth and ashes strategy?"

"The fishwife is not around," I explained, before I told her about what I heard Mrs. King say to her son.

"Wow!" she breathed. "What are you going to do?"

"I don't know yet."

"To be honest, she sounds like a true psychopath. You know, divide and rule. I know you want to help, but maybe the King family is not your problem. There are all kinds of bad situations going on in the world right now."

"I know, but I'm not stuck right in the middle of them." I couldn't get my mind off the King family members. Zackary's innocent vulnerability ... his father's terrible and needless isolation, and his mother's cruel deception. All of it saddened me and made me feel helpless.

"How are things with your ward's father?"

"Why would you ask me that?" I shot back guiltily.

April looked at me with narrowed eyes. "Er ... because you spoke about his *voice*. Have you had any more *interactions* with him?"

"Weren't you the one ready to screw my head off for even making such a statement?"

"Well after what you've told me about his wife and their marriage, that doesn't stand anymore."

"It still does in my book," I said, "and moreover I haven't got to see him properly yet."

"I know the burns are probably a serious situation, but the mask makes him sound so ... appealing. Does he wear it all the time?"

I felt myself blushing. "The mask covers half of his face."

"Why are you blushing?"

"I kind of saw him in the mirror."

"What? When were you planning on telling me that? Come on ... what does he look like?"

"He's ... he's ... he's beautiful, April."

She frowned. "Hang on. You just lost me. He's got such bad scars he has to wear a mask ..."

"Yes, he is badly scarred, but somehow they make him special. Oh, I know I'm not making any sense. I don't understand it myself, but they make him … do you know what I mean?"

"No, but tell me more."

"He has great abs too."

Her eyes popped open. "You've seen his abs?"

I nodded. "I had to take his breakfast tray to his room. He was shirtless."

"You're Zackary's nanny. What on earth are you doing carrying breakfast trays to his room?"

"It's a long story."

"I have time."

I sighed. "All right. The girl who was supposed to take it was not around and I volunteered okay?"

"You volunteered?"

"Uh … huh."

She grinned. "So how much did you actually see?"

"Just an outline," I said quickly. "The details were cast in shadows."

"Damn, I should pay a visit one of these days to your castle. I'm dying to have a glimpse. You know it's men like this that know exactly what they're doing. They're all dark and broody and then they pounce and rip your clothes to pieces …" She wiped invisible sweat off her brow. "God damn it's been a while since my husband did that. I'll have to rectify the situation as soon as I push this baby out."

I laughed. One of these days I will tell her what I really feel for Brett King.

"Just to make things clear do you have any plans on getting it on with Mr. Gazillionaire?"

I gave her a dry look. "What the hell is wrong with you? Is this actually coming from your mouth?"

"He's more or less divor—" she said.

"Actually, he's not." I felt the amusement and hilarity of the last few minutes drain away. The truth was no matter how it looked from the outside the arrangement they had set up worked for them and I was the outsider.

CHAPTER 30

CHARLOTTE

We got into Melly's Mini and she drove us to The Red Peahen. It was Melly's favorite bar. It seemed that out of all the others she had scoured, this was the one that seemed to draw the most handsome male patrons. All burly farmer types. I listened to her bright chatter, smiled encouragingly and made all the right noises, but quite honestly, the local eye-candy was the last thing on my mind.

It was Friday night so there was a small band playing in one corner and an area had been cleared in front to serve as a dance floor. Melly assured me it would be heaving later, but at the moment there wasn't a soul on it. The band was quite good though. They were playing old rock and roll numbers mixed in with a few sixties hits.

Melly bought the first round and we settled into our seats. She tossed an almond at me. "Is this how you're going to spend your night off?"

"What do you mean?"

"Like you dropped your pizza cheese down on the ground."

I grinned. "I'd still eat it."

"Don't tell anyone," she whispered dramatically, "but so would I."

After that we had quite a nice time and I ended up drinking far more than I normally would have. About nine-thirty a couple of guys walked in and Melly's mouth dropped open as she pushed her glass away from her. "Did you see that?"

I turned around. A brawny guy in faded jeans and a green shirt had just walked in and made his way to the bar.

I turned back to her. "Did you see the girl he's with?"

She made a face. "Never mind. That tall guy over there, three o'clock, has been staring at you. Do you want to go say hi or should I step in?"

I lifted my head and true enough, an attractive guy was sneaking looks our way. "Why do you have to make it happen?" I asked. "Let him come over if he's interested."

She sighed heavily. "In case you haven't noticed, gender expectations are now non-existent. Speaking about gender expectations I haven't had sex in months and I'd really like to get laid tonight."

Her eyes connected with a couple of guys standing at the bar she had identified earlier as potential partners. She rose to her feet with determination. "Does the guy in the black shirt seem like he'll do, or does Mr. Brown Boots beside him appear to have more potential?"

They were passable enough. Not really my type. My type was at the castle. "How am I supposed to know what'll do for you?" I could feel my words starting to slur. I knew I should stop drinking.

"I need to know who to invest my energy on. They came together so if I pick the wrong one I lose out on both."

"Black Shirt's got more guns ..."

"True," she agreed and emptied her glass in one smooth movement. Black Shirt stood to his feet then and she sucked in her breath. "Jesus, did you see the ass he's been sitting on all this time?"

Well, okay, I had to agree. Farmer Black Shirt was worth the walk up to the bar. "Go for it," I encouraged.

She was transfixed. "I am, but he's something to behold, isn't he?" She plopped back into her seat. "I think I'm intimidated."

I couldn't contain my amusement. "What happened to gender expectations and all that?" I asked. "You were never going to go up to either of them, were you? You're too chicken."

She scratched her head, and sent me a sheepish smile. "You may be right. I was hoping I'd be able to inspire you and you'd lead the way. I'm all talk, I guess. Can you believe I lost my virginity at twenty-seven? Yup, and to an asshole too. After waiting that long I thought I would see fireworks, but instead all I remember are the brown stains on his apartment ceiling from a water leak. I swear one of them was shaped like a giant dick."

It would have been funny if it was not so sad. Slamming my glass on the table I pulled her to her feet. I had a decent amount of drink in me so I just took a deep breath and headed over towards Black Shirt and his friend. To my great surprise and delight, his friend rose to meet me halfway, the kindest of smiles across his face.

"Hi," I said to him.

"Hey," he replied. "You have more guts than me."

"I'm just a bit more drunk."

He laughed, and I could feel the nervous tension within me begin to unravel. Maybe I could never have Brett King, but there was a sea of men out there for me. All I had to do was forget him. And what better way than with such a sweet guy.

"Can you stomach one more drink?" he asked with a slow smile.

The band was playing *Great Balls Of Fire*. There was still no one on the dance floor yet, but what the heck. I smiled up at him. "A dance for now sounds amazing. The drink can come after."

"As you wish ..." he said gallantly, and taking my hand twirled me to the dancefloor. I dragged Melly with me. I was going to get her Black Shirt for her, or die trying. I glanced back and sure enough Black Shirt was watching us. I began to believe it had been a good call to come out this evening.

No matter what, I was going to forget Brett King ... and his fabulous abs.

CHAPTER 31

BRETT

I had spent the last four hours restless and angry. I hadn't felt this way for a long time. In the end I had tried to burn off the excess energy by training for nearly two hours. My muscles were screaming as I stepped into a hot shower. I toweled my hair as I walked to my trio of computer screens. I would work until I became so exhausted I could no longer keep my eyes open. Work always took me to a place where no other thoughts could come in.

I looked at the numbers on the screen. Usually, that would have been enough to pull me into another world, but tonight I could not get into it. I looked at the clock. Nearly eleven. I stood and went to the bar. I poured myself a very large scotch and downed it in one. The liquid radiated warmth all the way down to my stomach.

I sighed. I knew what was wrong with me. It burned me to look down from my window and see Charlotte leave with Melly. I knew what two girls out on the town did. And Charlotte looked beautiful in a pink, figure hugging sweater and jeans that showed off her curves. It maddened me to think of all the men who would look at her. It maddened me even more to think I had no right over her. As much as I wanted it she was not mine. If she saw my face …

Fuck.

My fist slammed into the palm of my left hand. I poured myself another glass. What if she went home with another man? Jesus Christ, I couldn't believe I was torturing myself like this. Angrily, I paced the floor. Last orders were at 10.00. The pubs started throwing people out at 10.30. She should have been back by now.

I stopped mid-stride. What if they had met with an accident? Now, I was being paranoid.

I heard the sound of a car, and rushed to my window. I saw a taxi drive up to the gates and relief poured through my body. I wanted to stay at the window and watch her come in, but I forced myself to walk away. I sat at my computer and stared at the screen while my ears strained to hear the sounds in the courtyard. I heard the sound of two doors slamming shut. I heard a giggle. Then it was quiet.

I let go of the breath I was holding. She was back. All was well.

I nearly jumped out of my skin when the intercom buzzed. "Charlotte?" I said.

"Brett, is that you?"

"Yes. Is everything alright?"

"No. I'm thinking of quitting."

Everything in me instantly stilled.

"Did you hear me?" she asked belligerently, her words slurring. "I'm thinking of … of … quitting."

I exhaled with relief. Charlotte Conrad was intoxicated.

"Why do you want to quit?" I asked, prepared to be entertained.

Something fell to the ground and she cursed. "I want to quit because I cannot stand the way both of you treat Zackary. You ignore him. His mother feeds him a bunch of lies."

"What lies?"

"Oh that. I'll have to talk to you about them later."

"Why?"

"Because … because it's very important and I need to be sober, you know what I mean?"

"Yes."

"I mean, I know that things aren't easy but … you're not even trying anymore."

Again I heard the clatter of something falling and another low curse. I tried not to laugh. "Sit on your bed," I suggested. All the noise was probably her struggling to remain upright. She was so drunk it was a wonder she was still able to communicate.

"I'm sitting now. That was a good idea, Brett. Anyway, coming back to what I was saying. What was I saying? Oh yeah, you are not trying anymore. I expect better from you, Brett King."

"Why?"

"I don't know," came her response. I knew without seeing her that she was frowning. And I knew she would look adorable. "But I … I just know … you caaaaaan."

"Will you stay if I say I'll try harder?"

"I guess so."

A brief silence ensued. "Where have you been tonight?"

"The Red Something. Peahen … cockerel. Some sort of bird anyway." She burst out in giggles.

"Did you have a good time?"

"I drank a lot and I danced," she announced innocently, but the harmless information wound up all the nerves in my body. "There was a farmer there. He looked a bit like you," she added.

My snort was bitter. She knew nothing of what I looked like, but still I wanted to find out how she had imagined me to be in her mind. "What did he look like?"

"A little bit like you, slightly smaller and not as nice obviously, but in the dark, I could have been fooled. However, his voice … I hated it. Yours rumbles … it is low and sexy, his was a ring. I thought I'd suddenly developed that ear disease. What is it called? It's like a high-pitched ringing."

I smiled then. "Tinnitus."

"That's the one."

"Brett."

"Yes."

"I want to be *filled* again," she blurted out suddenly.

I froze. I didn't need an explanation to understand what she meant, especially at the way her voice became sultry and breathless on the last word.

She went on. "There's this constant, fluttering ache down in my—"

Her breathing hitched as though she wasn't even in control of her words.

She groaned. "It won't freaking stop. It's hollow and insatiable … and no matter how hard I try I just can't stop replaying that night."

The question was torn from my lips. "What night?"

"It was so real I still can't be sure if it actually happened, or if it was just a dream … but my God. You came at me … your tongue speared me … it was hot and wet … and so was I. Actually, I was soaked. That's a better term. Soaked. Your teeth bit down on my clit and I explo—"

I didn't wait to hear the rest. I was out of my room in an instant.

The lights had all been turned off for the night. The corridors were illuminated only by the external lights and the rays of moonlight. It didn't matter because I'd been wandering these corridors in the dark for years. I knew the path by heart.

CHAPTER 32

BRETT

https://www.youtube.com/watch?v=2i2khp_npdE
Sing Me To Sleep

As I hurried down the corridors, I asked myself what exactly I was going to do when I reached her. *It's just to ensure that she's alright,* came the response from inside my head. I pretended to believe it. I didn't allow myself to think of the consequences of my actions. Later. I will think of them later, but for now, pure unadulterated lust was my guiding light.

Blood raced through me and drummed in my ears. I didn't even knock, I just pushed the door open and walked through. She was settled on the floor, her legs pushed straight in front of her, and leaning against the bed.

I had not been with a woman in years so I just stood there and watched her. Not just watched, I drank her in. Every last detail.

From the gentle sway of her head nodding to a tune in her head only she could hear, to the soft tilt of her lips in a dreamy smile. My eyes noted that her sweater was the same sweet pink of her lipstick. The neckline had been pulled down by her hunched position and I could see the creamy wing-like protrusions of her collar bone.

In the yellow light her skin looked like silk and the need to taste it overwhelmed me. I wanted to lick that warm, soft skin. She started to rise then, her movements unstable. Instantly, I went to her. With both of my hands grasping her upper arms I pulled her upright and watched as her eyes focused on me.

Damn she was beautiful.

"Hey," she said softly. "Have you come to help me get into bed?"

"Yes." My voice was almost a growl of frustration. Pushing the covers aside, I lowered her on the bed. She still had her heels on so I took her foot in my hand and began to undo the buckles. They were fiddly. My big hands looked clumsy.

"You don't need to undo them, just pull them off," she said.

I grasped the heel and pulled the first one off. My gaze trans-fixed on the gentle pink of her toe nails. Helplessly, my fingers traced the fine net of blood vessels. Her skin was warm and soft. So soft I wanted to lay my cheek against it.

My hand lingered on her skin … brushing across it ever so lightly, my heart flooding with warmth at the idea of being able to care for her in this way. If only I could. But of course, I couldn't. She was not going to want me, not once she sees my face. I put her foot down and picked up the other. I stroked it. She was so gone she would almost definitely not remember any of this, which would be a good thing. She was Zackary's nanny. She was out of bounds to me.

However, the monster in my pants was agonizing to ignore.

With a sigh, I took off her shoe and straightened. She looked up at me, and writhed her body upon the bed. There was a knowing, inviting smile on her face.

"Will you stay, Brett?" Her voice trembled with emotion.

I was shaking my head when her hand slipped down slowly. From her stomach down to the waistband of her jeans.

My jaw clenched as I watched transfixed, as she tried to slip her hands further down, but couldn't get past the barrier her jeans presented.

That was my cue. I turned away before I lost my mind, determined to head to the door; however, as I reached it, I heard a soft moan leave her lips. I came to a halt. I wanted to leave … it was the right thing to do, but her body. Her heat. The lure of her perfume haunted me.

With my back to her, I switched off the light, but her words were still playing in my head.

your tongue speared me …
I'm still not sure if it actually happened, or if it was just a dream

I turned around and went back to stand over her.

"Please," she begged huskily.

I wanted to take her. Hell, I was desperate to have her, but no matter how much I craved her, I wasn't going to take her while she was this drunk. She could barely stand.

"I can't take advantage of you while you're like this," I said harshly. "It's not fair."

"You don't understand," she whispered. "I can only have you while I am like this. And I really do want you. All the time. Day and night."

I wanted to believe her. How I wanted to, but I couldn't do it. I didn't move. I stood as still as a statue.

"Then just watch me," she said, her hand was once again finding its way downwards.

I watched, as she swirled her hips to the delicious circling of her clit. A frustrated frown appeared on her forehead while she tried unsuccessfully to unbutton her jeans. Fuck, I felt the same frustration. Without thinking, I bent down and slipped the button out of its hole.

The sound of the zip echoed inside me. I swallowed. It had been so damn long.

With both her hands she tugged her jeans down revealing white cotton underwear with little bears on it. I felt my heart lurch at her innocence. Jillian would have died before wearing something like that. I lost track of my thoughts as her hand dived underneath the cheap material. Her movements were honest, almost as if she was unaware of my prying eyes. A painful shot of desire raced through my veins.

I was so hard it hurt. It killed me to watch her and yet I couldn't take my eyes off her.

She only managed a few thrusts before her intoxication overwhelmed her. To my shock I found myself falling to my knees. My lips found their way to the skin just below her belly button.

Her scent and the warmth instantly wiped any remnants of logic from my head. My tongue slipped out to taste her. Pushing her top higher, I speared the tip into her navel, and her body arched with pleasure.

Her hands cradled my masked face. I instantly flinched at the unfamiliar contact. I lifted my eyes to her face and saw her eyes were still shut. Taking a deep breath, I found a way to relax as she lightly ran her fingers upwards until they were in my hair.

"Please. Let me come, Brett," she urged.

I threw away reason and crushed my mouth to the protruding nub. Breathing in the heady scent of her, I licked her clit through the cotton material. Her moan rang out into the silent night. Positioning myself properly between her hips, I slid the crotch of her panties to one side and looked at her glistening pink flesh.

"I will go to hell for this," I muttered, as I buried my head between her thighs and sucked the swollen lips of her sex into my mouth.

"Oh, Brett," I heard her call, and it swelled my chest with so much emotion that it was hard to breathe. She wasn't hoping it was anyone else. Even in her inebriated state I was the one on her mind. The danger of what that really entailed flashed in a corner of my mind, but I didn't want to deal with that. Not now.

I ravaged her pussy like a starving man, my tongue licking

every sweet fold, and my teeth nipping at her engorged flesh. Deep almost unrecognizable growls rumbled from within my throat. My dick felt like it was on the verge of exploding, and I wanted to thrust it into her delicious pussy. To feel the fingers that were pulling on my hair, clawing down the bare skin of my back. To fill her up to bursting just as she had wished.

I wanted to fulfill her request more than I wanted to take my next breath.

Pulling away, I slipped a finger inside of her, and then a second. I felt her walls convulse around me. With the pad of my thumb circling her clit, I thrust voraciously in and out of her ... goading her climax. She shot up from the bed as a storm of ecstasy ripped through her, her entire body thrashing. I pulled my head away to watch the result of my onslaught.

"*Fuck,*" she cursed, her body arching uncontrollably and her eyes wide open. The waves passed and she lay back and looked at me with heavy lidded eyes.

"Brett ..." she called.

I went for her lips, kissing her deeply. She clung onto my neck as I drank her in. As if she really cared.

When I pulled away, she collapsed back unto the bed, her eyes shut and the most beautiful satisfied smile spread across her face. I was dying to have her, to let myself come, but she looked as if she had already fallen asleep. I got up from the bed and gazed down at her. For a few seconds I just watched her sleeping. So innocent. So beautiful. Then I quickly pulled her panties and jeans back in place. I didn't zip her up.

She never woke up.

I took my leave then, wondering just how much clarity she would be able to recall of all that had just happened. The taste of the alcohol she had consumed mixed with the earthy scent of her juices was in my mouth and I relished it.

I returned to my suite, and laid like a tormented man on my bed.

Fisting my cock I pumped myself to climax, my mind and heart on Charlotte's open pink pussy. If she ever became mine …

CHAPTER 33

CHARLOTTE

I stood in front of my bathroom mirror the next morning, my head throbbing, my mouth painfully parched, and stared at my eyes smeared with liner and mascara. I tried to recall the night. Melly and I ended up drinking Tequila shots with the two guys. Oh no! I suddenly remembered dancing on the table. Oh, my God, the bartender had to help me down. And oh shit, I fell into his arms. I pressed my palms to my cheeks with shame. The whole pub had cheered and laughed.

I frowned. What happened after that?

I could vaguely remember telling Melly my knees wouldn't work, and a hazy recollection of staggering out into the cool air. After that it was a complete blank. I couldn't for the life of me remember how we got back to the castle, or how I got to bed.

I jumped at the sound of the intercom. It was my day off so really, I could ignore it, but what if it was Brett or something urgent? My head was killing me so I turned slowly and walked towards it.

The hammering in my head made it hard for me to even bear the bright light. On the other end was Melly.

"Hey," she called.

"Please don't shout," I warned, holding my temples. My God, how could she sound so bright and cheerful?

"Uh … okay. What's wrong?"

"I'm just hungover. How did we end up back here?"

"Wait! You don't remember?"

"The last thing I remember is … getting out of the pub."

"Well that was what we did. We got into a taxi."

"We did?"

"Yup … the taxi driver was about a hundred years old and you were flirting with him. Incoherently though."

"And you let me …"

"I was drunk too."

"It's horrible that I can't remember anything. I'm never drinking Tequila again."

She laughed. "You should have done what I did. I took two headache tablets before I went to sleep."

"Yeah well, I didn't."

"Ah, it's your day off. What does it matter? No harm done."

I wanted to believe her that no harm had been done, but memories that I couldn't quite get a grasp of fleeted around my consciousness. I ended the call, popped two headache tablets, then lay on my bed and tried to remember what had happened after I had arrived. I fell asleep and woke up again an hour later feeling more human again.

As I stripped off in the bathroom, I looked down at myself and noted that something felt off. I felt sore between my legs … and strangely sated. As though … my heart lurched in my throat. Surely, nothing happened in the pub with the nice guy. No, I wouldn't have. Anyway, I could remember everything until I staggered out of the pub.

I tore off my panties and examined them. Then to be sure, I brought them to my nose and sniffed, but it did not smell foreign. But the sensation between my legs.

I ran out of the bathroom and called Melly on the intercom, my heart pounding in my chest. "What happened with the guy I was dancing with?"

"Actually, you ditched him after a few drinks … something about his voice?"

"Are you sure I ditched him?"

"Yup."

"Did I meet up with another guy?"

"Nope. By then you were pushing them all away with a stick you found on the floor."

"I didn't leave your sight for even a moment, right?"

"You didn't. That much I remember. I wasn't as drunk as you were, I remember everything."

"Alright," I said and ended the call.

Convincing myself to think nothing of my sensitive clit and sensation that something had happened, I headed into the shower and held my head under the running cascade. Maybe I had another wet dream.

I was soon dressed and on my way down the stairs.

I had only been really drunk three times in my life, but never ever so inebriated that I had suffered a complete blackout. Perhaps if I thought hard enough, whatever memories I couldn't remember would return to me in fragments.

I was just about to take out a slice of bread from the toaster when Mrs. Blackmore walked into the kitchen. She was startled to see me.

"What are you doing here so early? Aren't you supposed to be away?"

Her abrupt halt almost sent Mr. Boothsworth crashing into her. He quickly caught himself.

He smiled slyly. "Ah, you're up? Rough night, wasn't it?"

"What do you mean?"

He laughed. "Don't you remember? You were so drunk last night you almost tumbled down the stairs."

My mouth dropped open because I had absolutely no memory.

"I would have caught you don't worry," he said. "Anyway, I helped you to your room."

"What did I say?" I asked.

"You don't remember?"

I shook my head.

He laughed. "The almighty black out. It's been a few decades since any of those paid me a visit."

Mrs. Blackmore looked at me with horror on her face. "Why were you that drunk?"

I shook my head in bewilderment. "You didn't say much," Barnaby responded. "You just mumbled that you needed to call Brett … I'm assuming you meant Mr. King."

My eyes widened then in shock and so did Mrs. Blackmore's. "Did you call him in that state?"

I slapped my hands to my head then, and turned away from the both of them. Jesus, my heart was hammering in my chest. "Of course not," I answered automatically, but I knew it was a lie. Fragments of what I had done were already flooding back into my head.

"Well, you'll never know," Mr. Boothsworth said cheerfully.

I was so horrified I wanted to cry. I grabbed my slice of toast and began to stuff it down my throat without even buttering it.

"Make her something," Mr. Boothsworth said.

Mrs. Blackmore came over to place her hands on my shoulders. Leading me towards the counter, she sat me down on a stool. "Does chicken soup sound good?"

I couldn't speak. I just nodded with gratitude. At that moment the intercom buzzed. Mr. Boothsworth went to answer it.

"Sir …" he said.

I swear I stopped breathing.

"I'll be right there," he said as I forced my half-chewed food down my throat.

"Was that Mr. King?" I croaked.

"Yes, he's just about to leave. I'll go and see him off."

I hurried to the window. A black Rolls Royce with tinted windows was waiting outside the front door. The window rolled down as Mr. Boothsworth hurried up to the car. I saw him at the window. He had his mask on. He spoke quietly to his butler.

I saw Mr. Boothsworth step away, and suddenly Brett slid his gaze over and looked directly at me. In a fraction of an instant another memory filled my head. Was it real? I couldn't be sure, but I could feel the heat rushing up my throat and into my face. I nodded my head slightly in greeting and hoped he couldn't see how red I was from that distance. The smile he gave me almost made my heart stop. Then the window rolled back up and he was driven away, as sleek as a dream.

CHAPTER 34

CHARLOTTE

Zackary returned to the house at noon.

I was awoken by warm breath on my face. When I opened my eyes, my heart sang with joy when I met his bright blue eyes and sleekly combed hair staring back at me.

But I pretended as if he had scared the living daylights out of me. With my hand on my chest, I shot out of bed. "Oh my. That was scary," I cried and he dissolved into peals of laughter. Mrs. Blackmore smiled at my antics.

"Why are you here?" I asked, surprised but very happy to see him back. I had grown to love him so quickly. Maybe it was because I have never taken care of a child with such a sad and vulnerable face.

The housekeeper made a face behind his back. "His mother had a change of plans so he was sent back. She has a function in Frankfurt and his aunt is too old to be with him on her own."

"Well, lucky me then," I cried and drew his smiling innocent face into my arms for a hug. When I pulled away I saw that his face was screwed up in half-hearted distaste, but I considered it a victory. He did not pull away or rearrange his hair.

"Lunch is almost ready so you can both head down to the kitchen in about half an hour. Do you feel better, Charlotte?"

I nodded and she left.

"What do you want to do?" I asked.

"Can we fly the kite today?"

"Well, we won't have enough time. We need to be back for lunch in thirty minutes," I replied.

His face fell then. "Awww …"

"How about we read together for a few minutes, hmmm?"

"Okay," he agreed reluctantly. We read for twenty minutes then we went downstairs to the dining room to await his meal.

"I saw your father today."

I watched him very carefully, and saw his eyes fill with a mixture of curiosity, fear, and sadness.

"What is it Zackary?" I asked as gently as possible.

"I haven't seen him in a long, long time."

"Do you want to see him?"

A hundred different emotions seemed to cross his face in that moment, and for the longest time he didn't say a word.

"Zackary?" I prompted

He turned his head towards me then and I saw the tears well up in his beautiful eyes.

Maybe I shouldn't have pushed so quick. "Zackary?"

"He makes me afraid," he said.

My heart felt as if it was breaking. For both father and son.

"Why?" I asked.

"He is a monster."

I recognized the word his mother had used, and my temper flared. I took a very deep and long breath. "Why would you say that?"

"His face is very ugly."

"His face is that way because of the accident."

The moment I said that he searched my gaze earnestly. As if he was desperate to believe something other than what he had been told. His innocence touched me deeply.

"You know that your father was involved in a very terrible accident, right?"

He nodded.

"Well, he sustained many injuries to his face so he doesn't look like most people, but he is not a monster. He is just ..." I couldn't find the right words. "Have you ever seen the scars on his face, Zackary?"

He shook his head. "No, he wears a mask. Mummy says the scars underneath are too horrid and frightening."

I thought of what I could say then and my mind went to the

burn scar on my wrist. "Here …" I said to him. "I got this when I was just a bit older than you. I was trying to make it better for my Mummy by ironing some clothes for her, but I didn't understand how hot the iron was so I burned myself. The wound healed but look at the scar that is left."

He gazed at it for the longest time and I stayed completely silent.

"Does it hurt?" he asked finally.

"Not anymore, but it was extremely painful when it happened. I cried for hours and hours. My Daddy had to put ice on it and everything."

"Can I touch it?"

"If you want."

He reached out and touched it, his chubby little fingers going over the raised white skin. His face was thoughtful and I waited a few seconds to let the message sink in before I spoke again.

"If I had two more of these would it make me a monster?"

He thought about it, then shook his head.

"What about if I had ten more, Zackary?"

This time he didn't have to think about it. He shook his head immediately.

"It is the same with your father. He is not a monster just because he has a few scars on his face."

"But he is always angry with Mummy."

I shook my head. "No, he's not."

He nodded. "Yes, he is. He makes her very sad because he wants to take me away from her."

I didn't know where to start. It was such a pack of lies. "None of that is true …" I couldn't help myself from saying.

His response was to frown. "Mummy said," he insisted stubbornly.

If I was not careful I was going to get myself in big trouble. "I'm not saying that she lied or anything like that. Maybe it was just a misunderstanding … you know. Sometimes adults get it wrong too."

Mrs. Blackmore arrived with Zackary's lunch then, and I turned to take the tray from her. "Thank you," I said with a smile. As I put the meal before him, I quietly shot my last bullet. "Your father loves you very much, and he would love to spend some time with you, so do not be scared of him, alright?

"What about Mummy? I think she might not like it if I chose Daddy instead of her."

"How about we let Daddy handle Mummy?"

He nodded eagerly, and I fell a little bit more in love with him.

CHAPTER 35

CHARLOTTE

I remembered the kiss …

Everything else was vague and dreamlike, but the kiss was vivid. I could still taste it. It was the kind of deep kiss, I imagined when I was child, had been given to Snow White or Sleeping Beauty. It had everything. Passion, romance … great love. It was so similar to the first night I'd been at the house, and yet so different. These memories refused to fade … flashing into my mind, then disappearing before I could grab a hold of them.

Of course, it couldn't possibly have happened. There was no way.

After I put Zackary to sleep I came down to sit with Carrie and Mrs. Blackmore. We passed the late evening away in the warmth of the kitchen with cups of tea, scones and the uncomplicated conversation of simple working people. These were my kind of people.

Both women laughed and reacted to the drama that they

were watching on TV, but my mind was engaged in trying to retrieve the events from the night before.

Surreal fragments of being touched in secret places came to me, the reminder of sheets being pulled away from my body. An underlying note of excitement accompanied these memories. The pit of my stomach was fluttering with nerves and it kept me tense.

The memory of a pair of gray eyes watching me.

His tongue had been in me … I was sure of it … I felt it, and as I tightened my hold on the handle of my cup I felt my hand tremble.

What exactly had happened?

The door suddenly opened and all the hair on my body stood to attention before I even turned to see why it was. Both Mrs. Blackmore and Carrie jumped to their feet. "Mr. King," they called in unison.

Tea splashed from my cup, I jumped to my feet along with them and turned around to meet the gray eyes that had haunted me all day. He appeared dark and imposing in a light blue, bishop-collared dress shirt, dark slacks and his mask.

I broke his gaze and lowered my face to the floor.

"Do you need Barnaby, Sir?" Mrs. Blackmore asked. She sounded flustered. "He headed off into town to meet with a friend."

"No, I don't need him."

Mrs. Blackmore glanced at me and Carrie nervously. "Is there anything I can get you, Sir?"

"Some fruit and tea," he said slowly.

I risked a look at him and found his gaze blatantly and unashamedly on me. I could feel both Carrie and Mrs. Blackmore watching the both of us with unbridled interest.

"I'll get it delivered as soon as it's ready," Mrs. Blackmore said quickly.

The source of my nightmare and fantasies nodded and took his leave.

Mrs. Blackmore heaved a sigh of relief, her shoulders slumping from being so nervous.

"Oh, my God. I can't believe he came in here," Carrie gasped.

"Will you take the tray up to him, Carrie?" Mrs. Blackmore asked, as she bustled around preparing his tea.

"I'll take it up to him," I said, before my brain got involved.

Both women turned to look at me.

"I'd like to speak to him about Zackary," I said quickly.

"I don't think you're going to get very far doing it one to one," Carrie said. "He doesn't speak much at all. I've attended to his wing for a long time now, and I think this was the first time I've heard him speak directly to another human being."

"It wouldn't hurt to try," I said with a shrug.

"So what do you think of him?" Carrie asked. "Is this the first time you've seen him in real life?"

"He's very imposing," I said truthfully.

Carrie nodded in agreement. "I've got no arguments there. In my first few months working in his wing I was too scared to even look him in the eye. The way that Madam spoke of him, I really thought he was some kind of monster ready to bite my head off, but really, he's quite the mysterious knight, almost like a romantic hero from a novel, is he not, Mrs. Blackmore?"

"Dashing is the word you're looking for," she said. "He makes me think of the many sweaty nights in my youth."

Carrie giggled. "I completely agree. I can't believe Madam goes to other men when there's more than enough to keep her busy at home. Sometimes I just want to give him a big heartfelt hug. All those scars and living all on his own up there. Charles, who used to work here as a chauffeur, said there were many nights he heard the master screaming in pain as he forced himself to learn to walk again."

The kettle that had been placed to boil on the stove sounded off, and Mrs. Blackmore immediately busied herself with making the tea. Carrie helped her cut up a selection of fruit.

"There you go," Mrs. Blackmore said, putting a small vase of flowers on the tray.

I drained my cup and picked up the tray. Things hadn't gone so well the last time I was there, so as I approached his door I took deep even breaths to steady my nerves.

His door was left partly open so after one knock, I walked in and settled it on the table by his door. As I straightened, he emerged from the room.

His eyes.

In that moment, I knew he had been with me the previous night. I felt hot color flood my face and my big plans to ask him to confirm or deny what had happened last night shattered. Maybe this was a bad idea. "Right. I'll see you later," I said, and like a little coward turned away to leave.

"Stay," he ordered.

I stopped in my tracks and faced him.

CHAPTER 36

CHARLOTTE

He cocked his head and watched me, his eyes roving down my body with an expression I had never seen before. There was confidence and a new possessiveness there. There was also a knowing. I felt bare and stripped naked before his look. Just then the memory of his face between my legs came to me out of nowhere, and my eyes popped open in disbelief. *Was I going crazy?*

Surely that didn't happen? I swallowed hard and tried not to show how affected I was by him.

His gaze burned a hole through me, but I continued to keep eye contact even when he came very close to me. He was so close I felt his heat like a living breathing thing. With a fork he picked up a piece of persimmon, his movements unhurried, but each second ticked away in my head like a bomb. The fruit slipped between his lips. I had a flash of seeing his lips shiny with juices. My juices.

I dropped his gaze then. I could have sworn he was doing it deliberately, to torture me, but all I could do was play along. I didn't know what had happened last night and I needed him to tell me.

"I want to *fuck* you. What's it going to take?"

Time slowed down. My heart lurched in my throat and I felt all the breath drain out of my body. I was sure that I had not heard him right.

"What?"

Patiently, he repeated himself. "I want to *fuck* you. What's it going to take?"

True, I was shocked since I was not expecting him to be so blunt, but I also felt an undeniable flare of desire at the raw hunger I saw in his eyes.

"But you're married," I whispered.

Something flashed in his eyes. "Is it a divorce you need?"

Hearing him say the word confused me. I frowned. "No, I mean … I don't know. I don't want to be the person who breaks up a family. I couldn't live with myself."

His lips twisted. "You call what I have a family? To all intents and purposes I am alone, Charlotte."

"What about Jillian?"

"What about Jillian?" he sneered. "Do you know where she is now?"

I shook my head.

"She is in London with one of her many lovers."

I bit my bottom lip. Of course she was. "What about

Zackary?"

I saw a flash of sadness in his eyes. "I will keep Zackary with me. Jillian is welcome to visit him as much as she wants, or he can go and stay with her for a weekend, but there is no way I am giving him up."

"She's not going to allow it."

"She won't have a choice. I am not taking Zackary with me to punish her. He is not even my biological son. I am taking him because it is the best thing I can do for him."

I stared at him in shock. Finally, it clicked. That was why he looked nothing like Brett and everything like his mother.

"So, back to my original question …"

"I'm not a toy," I lashed out. "Or a game that you can just play with and discard."

"I never said you were." His eyes narrowed. "You want me too … so what's the problem?"

"How can you be so damn sure I want you?"

"My tongue was in your cunt last night. You came with my fingers inside you, calling out my name … no one else's."

My jaw dropped. What the hell? I came with his fingers inside me? The only flashbacks I had was of him eating me out.

"You don't remember any of it?" His eyes showed genuine astonishment.

But I couldn't believe it either. My employer came to my room and did, God knows what, to me while I was practically unconscious. "You did … things to me while I was incoherent?" I whispered in disbelief.

He jerked back, his eyes tormented. "What? No! Don't you remember? You called me and told me about your dream. You wanted me to fill you up."

I shut my eyes. Yes, yes, I did remember. Oh, God! I did do that. What a fool I'd made of myself last night, and again, by not even remembering asking someone to have sex with me.

"Do you want me to elaborate further?"

When I couldn't respond he went on.

"You begged me, Charlotte."

"For fucks sake stop it!" I yelled, not because what he was saying wasn't true, but because I was horribly ashamed of how I had thrown myself at him like some cheap slut. My first instinct was to run away from him and hide my shame. I whirled around and started running.

"Let me go," I cried but he spun me around and imprisoned my arms by my sides.

"Charlotte."

"Let me go, otherwise this won't end here."

"It better not," he snarled. "Look at me. Fucking look at me."

I did and I couldn't breathe. The expression in his eyes tore at my insides. The maddening longing for him came back, but knowing we had done intimate things that I had no memory of embarrassed and crippled me. Made me unable even to think.

"You can sue me if you want …" he rasped, "for however much

you think it's worth and I'll pay you every dime, but I won't apologize for last night. I want you. I've always wanted you, and I always will. Maybe it was a mistake for you." He paused. "Tell me why are you rejecting me, Charlotte. Don't lie to me. Whatever it is I'll accept it."

I was about to dismiss the question and fight for my release from him when the significance of his question struck me. I stared at his face. His incredibly beautiful face. I could not understand how anyone could even think to call this man a monster. Even with the trace of scars running down from under his eyes he still looked more beautiful than most men I had ever come across. I told him the truth.

"It's not because of your scars."

He had been ready for the blow, for what he was sure was the reason for my rejection, but when he heard my statement, his guard slipped for just a moment. And for a second I saw the terrible sadness and loneliness within. I was no longer intimidated by him ... or embarrassed that I had begged him to have sex with me. In that moment, I wanted more than anything in the world to embrace him and try to make up for the pain that he'd had to endure. For the suffering ridicule and rejection he'd suffered at Jillian's hands.

The moment was fleeting.

Before I could even respond to him, he had put the steel back into his gaze. "Then why?" he growled.

There was only one reason, but it was something I could not see past. No matter what he said, he could never change the fact that as far as Zackary was concerned I would always be the other woman. He would never understand. He would learn to hate me. He would think I had pretended to love him, and then torn his family up from the inside. The end would surely be drastic.

"I don't owe you an explanation," I said to him but before I could leave he slid a hand around my neck and crushed my lips to his.

I fought the kiss ... pulling my mouth from his, but it still ended up back where it seemingly belonged. His slanted lips fit my mouth perfectly, wrenching more emotion from me than should have been possible.

I pushed at his shoulders, but with his hands around my waist he held me in place until his tongue slid into my mouth. Then my entire body went limp. There was no more fight in me. I gave in to pleasure. He stroked and dipped, and sucked, and I totally surrendered to the delicious assault. He tasted heavenly, but at the same time beautifully sinful. He was mine and yet he was forbidden. I couldn't place a reason on it. More than anything I wanted to understand why I reacted to him in this way.

His lips withdrew from mine.

"Brett," I croaked, my brain starting to reassert itself.

Instead of answering me, his mouth claimed my neck. A ripple of sweet ecstasy coursed through me. It made my toes curl. I snaked my hands around his neck and let my fingers tangle in his hair. I gasped when my back was slammed against a wall.

We needed to stop otherwise I would lose myself, I thought. But I didn't do anything about it. I just let the passion in me build higher and higher and grow even wilder. Suddenly, an image of Zackary crying for his mother came into my head. I felt something like panic and tears rushed to my eyes as I struggled to break free of him.

If I didn't let go now, I would never be able to. "Brett," I cried, "Brett. Stop."

My voice reverberated in the still room and he immediately came to a halt. His breathing was ragged, and so was mine. He lifted his gaze to mine and seeing the tears in my eyes, flinched and pulled away from me.

I felt cold when the heat of his body was gone. So cold I wanted to throw myself back into his embrace.

"Charlotte, are you alright?" he started to reach out, but I held my hand out. "Please don't touch me."

I couldn't meet his eyes for the fear that he would see how much I wanted him. I hurried away from the room.

CHAPTER 37

BRETT

It was barely a day later when Jillian stormed into my office.

She was fuming as she approached. I leaned back into my seat and watched her explode in a way that only Jillian could. "What the fuck is this?"

She flung the folder on the table, and the stack of papers inside scattered out. I watched calmly as they floated down and landed in varying locations across the table and the floor. There was not a stitch of makeup on her face and for a moment it took me back to when we were younger.

"You're asking for a divorce?" she screeched. "Where the hell is this coming from?"

"Don't you think it's high time we bring our joke of a relationship to an end?" I asked her quietly.

"Who says it's a joke," she yelled at me. "Who? Why is it a joke?"

"Are we truly married, then?" I asked.

For a moment she was at a loss for words, then she took a deep breath to calm herself. "Brett, we're fine. We have an agreement. An arrangement that gives Zackary stability and access to both his parents. Cancel this rubbish."

"I'm not fine. The agreement doesn't suit me anymore," I said to her. "You sleep around ... get into accidents that I constantly have to clean up ... ignore our child. What then is your use to me exactly?"

"This has been going on for years and you've never said a word. Why is it bothering you now?"

"It's high time we made a clean bre—"

"Is there someone else?" she cut in, her eyes glittering. "You've been indifferent all along. I cannot understand why you are suddenly in such a hurry to be free."

"What part of living this way are you okay with?"

"It doesn't matter," she cried. "We have almost everything. You have more money than you could ever be able to spend even if you lived to be a thousand. You have the prestige. Very few men in this world hold as much influence as you do. What else do you fucking want?"

I watched her carefully. "What does any of this have to do with my wanting a divorce?"

"I grew up with you, Brett. My father was more yours than he ever was to me. I should have had a problem with that, but it didn't matter because I knew you had nothing. I cared about you."

"Spare me. You didn't give a damn about your father."

"Take that back, Brett King. I loved my father until you ripped me away from him."

"He wanted you to marry me, or have you forgotten?"

"He would turn in his grave if he knew what you got up to in London."

"I do it because I am unhappy," she cried.

"Look, I really don't care anymore. I don't want to be married to you anymore."

"Please, Brett."

"Why do you want to be married to someone who doesn't want you?"

"Are you really that dense? With your last fucking name I am somebody. Do you think all those fine Lords and Ladies would give a shit about me if I was a divorcee? You expect me to give all that up for no reason?"

"Do you truly feel no shame when you mention any of this?" I should be used to her selfishness by now, but it appeared she still had the ability to surprise me.

"What shame?" she spat. "These are facts. I grew up with you and my father promising me the world and now you want to pull it out from under my feet. Not on your life."

I smiled cynically. "So, I'm more or less your trophy?"

"I don't give a damn what you call it, but no other woman will ever take my place. It is mine. You have refused to fix us, so you have to live with whatever is left."

I straightened. As far as I was concerned the performance

had come to an end. I picked up my office phone. "Barnaby, can you get the helicopter ready for me, please?"

"Yes, Mr. King," came the response.

"Brett, we're not done."

"I am," I snarled. "Get out of my office, and make sure to sign those papers before I tear everything apart."

Tears of self-pity filled her eyes. "I'll take Zackary away from you. I swear it."

My response was simple. "Try."

CHAPTER 38

CHARLOTTE

T he knock on my door made me jump. When it creaked open to reveal Zackary's scared small face I shot out my hand to call him to me. He ran to me, a fire truck in his hand, and I pulled him up to sit on my lap.

"Are you alright?" I asked.

He shook his head, tears in his eyes. I embraced him, perfectly understanding why. The whole place was in a commotion because Jillian was throwing a drunken tantrum. She had returned suddenly a little while before dinner and tore through the house smashing things and cursing like a sailor.

Since then it had been nothing but screams of fury, and the smashing of things either to the ground or against walls, alarming movements, and thuds that no one could decipher.

Mr. Boothsworth had gone up to attend to her, but he remained outside her door, as she would not let anyone in.

From her cursing and swearing I could almost suspect what

was happening, but I couldn't believe it, or rather I was too scared to. I had not forgotten Brett asking me if it was his divorce that would pave the way for us.

Zackary cupped his hand over my ear. "Is Mummy mad with me?" he whispered.

"Of course not. You haven't done anything wrong, have you?"

He shook his head solemnly.

"There you go. She's just a little upset right now, but everything will be fine when Daddy comes home. Do you want to come outside with me to play for a little bit?"

He nodded, needing to be away from the racket just as much as I did. We headed hand in hand over to his new playground and whiled away an hour on the swings. He was building a mighty sandcastle in his play box when we heard the helicopter arrive in the distance. I decided to keep Zackary outside, so he didn't accidentally hear anything he shouldn't.

When the sound of police sirens came up the driveway not too long after, I made sure to keep Zackary with me until all had subsided.

"Have the police come to take Mummy away?" Zackary asked, his eyes enormous with fear.

"No, of course not. I think they've just come to help Mummy feel less upset."

He nodded gravely and carried on building his sandcastle. After the police had left I walked into the kitchen after sending Zackary up to wash his hands.

Mrs. Blackmore talked to me in hushed tones. "We don't know who called the police, but they took Mrs. King away for destruction of property. Apparently, she started her damaging rampage at the restaurant where she was lunching and carried on at the local bar."

"Wow," I said quietly.

She looked stumped as she stared into nothingness. "I don't understand what could make her get so mad like that. She's always been bad tempered, but never like this."

"You should have heard the way Mr. King spoke to her. He was furious," Carrie said. "So much so he even dealt with the cops himself. He promised them he would make good any damage she had caused. They wanted to breathalyze her, but he wouldn't allow them to. He had Mr. Boothsworth smuggle her quickly into the helicopter and off she went. I think they knew they had been outwitted, but they were a bit in awe of Mr. King."

I listened quietly, not knowing how I felt about it all. Things were spinning out of control and so quickly, I didn't know when something was going to fly out of nowhere and take me down. When I said no to Brett I was sure that my principles were more important than my own pleasure, but as the hours passed I became more and more confused and truly at a loss about what I should do.

Zackary came down, and immediately Mrs. Blackmore began to fuss over him. For the last two days, I had been allowing him to eat dinner in the kitchen instead of the big dining room that felt cold and impersonal. He sat down and quietly ate his dinner paying little attention to the cartoon that I turned on for him.

When it was time to retire for the day I headed to my room and sat on my bed, staring up at the intercom. Waiting but for what I wasn't sure. I had turned him down. What did I expect? He would come chasing after me! After a while I got up and headed over to the window, hoping to see his silhouette at his window just as I had multiple nights in the past.

But he never appeared, and his lights never came on.

My heart waited for a call to come from him until I eventually fell into a restless slumber. All I had were the memories of his touch, a bitter sweet company.

CHAPTER 39

A few more days passed, and there was no word from either Zackary's father or mother. I adhered to Zackary's schedule and we, the staff, were left to fend for ourselves. More than ever the house seemed eerily cold and forlorn.

More often than not I would catch myself staring at the intercom, or out of the window over at his darkened part of the wing and wonder when he would return. Often, I would think I had made a terrible mistake by turning him down. How could I have been so stupid to put someone else's happiness before my own? Then Zackary would smile at me in a certain way and I knew I had done the right thing.

No love is worth destroying a child for.

A week passed before Barnaby came into the kitchen with an important announcement. "Mr. King will be back tonight, Mrs. Blackmore. It will be way past midnight so perhaps make him something light to eat."

"I'll have to stay awake late again." Mrs. Blackmore groaned lightly, and turned to the basket of garlic that she was peeling.

I thought long and hard about it before I opened my mouth to speak. "I think I'll be up later today so if you prepare it, I'll warm it up, and take it to him."

"Are you sure, love?" she asked. "I can easily hand it over to Carrie to take since she's in charge of his wing, anyway."

I gave her a simple smile. "It's okay, I can do it for her."

"Alright," she said, her smile bright. "I'll have to explain to you how to warm it properly, though."

"Okay, show me later."

"You've also been quite withdrawn these past few days. Is everything alright?"

I nodded. "All is well. I've just had some things to think through."

"Well I'm here if you need me," she said with a sincere smile.

I smiled back in gratitude.

W hat seemed like many hours later, I was on my way to Mr. King's suite. I was sure I was courting fire, but still I couldn't stop myself.

I heard his voice before I knocked on the door. I couldn't make out what he was saying, but the deep and quiet rumble of his voice was more than enough to listen to. He spoke clearly and without hurry, as if the whole world was required to match his pace.

I knocked, and to my surprise he came to the door and pulled it open. When he saw me, he stopped, and a strange expression crossed his eyes.

"Sure," he said to the speaker on the phone, as his eyes bored into mine.

"I brought you some food," I murmured.

Without acknowledging my presence or words, he turned away. Leaving the door open he headed back into the room. He took a seat in the lounge chair and continued with his call while I followed Mrs. Blackmore's instruction and laid down his meal on his dining table.

As I waited for him to finish his call, I tried not to feel hurt that he didn't immediately disengage. I could hear that it was neither urgent nor important. He was forcing me, just like the rest of the world to go at his pace. Now, I was just another member of his staff.

Just as I was turning away to leave, he put the phone away and turned his attention to me. "I didn't expect you to still be here."

I had the choice to be snotty, or polite as my status required. I chose the latter route. It would clarify the message of what we currently were. He was my employer and I was one of his staff.

"I couldn't leave Zackary uncared for when both his mother and father were absent. I have already asked the agency to look for my replacement and they will send someone as soon as Madam returns. I promise that whoever the agency sends will be a great nanny, and she will love Zackary immensely."

"The way you throw around that word," he said bitterly. "Is love that cheaply acquired?"

"Not cheaply, but easily, especially when the recipient is a brave, beautiful child like Zackary. He steals hearts quite easily."

He didn't say a word, but continued to watch me.

"Do you know when … er … Madam will be back?"

He shrugged carelessly. "Madam is in a voluntary rehab facility so it is anyone's guess when she decides to call it a day."

I cleared my throat and stated my request. "Then could you perhaps, please, clear your schedule tomorrow after lunch? About two o'clock in the gazebo. Zackary wants to show you how he flies his kite."

I was sure he was going to say no so I quickly added. "Please make this happen even if it's for ten minutes. I have spoken to him and this is one case where his excitement to fly the kite trumps anything else. I think it would be a good time for you to reignite your relationship."

I turned around to leave then, and he didn't stop me. It broke my heart, but it was me who had made the choice.

My only hope was he would honor the request. Before I left, I was going to try my very best to ensure that Zackary began the process of getting over the unreasonable and warrantless fear of his father.

CHAPTER 40

BRETT

I couldn't remember the last time I felt this nervous.

I stood before the mirror in my walk-in closet. I dressed in a blue hoodie and dark slacks. It was a little past two. The time for my appointment with Zackary was here and all I could see in the mirror was the mangled skin that was still visible even when I wore the mask.

I closed my eyes and tried to block out the image of Zackary screaming and running away in fright. I wouldn't hold it against him if he did it again. He was just a kid, afraid of the monster his dad had become. Charlotte was right. It was time to try again. Especially now that Jillian was out of the house.

The alternative was Zackary would grow up like I did, without an actual parent to lean on. I was lucky I had Stanley to step in and guide me, but Zackary had no one. Just a selfish drunk for a mother.

Turning away from the mirror I headed out to the gazebo.

They were already there. It seemed as if they had had a picnic.

She was speaking to him, a smile on her face. He said something and she threw her head back in laughter. I felt my heart warm and expand. This was the woman for me.

Then she noticed me and so did Zackary. My eyes slid over to him and I watched his face. His whole body tensed. I could recall that expression from memory. Pure fear.

Charlotte rose to her feet as I arrived and invited me to take a seat between the both of them. For the first time in years I was facing my son. He was staring at me as one would a highly colored snake. Equal measure of fascination and fear.

I softened my voice as much as I could. "How are you, Zackary?"

He turned to Charlotte for reassurance and met a blinding smile and a nod to urge him on.

"Fine," he mumbled.

I smiled.

I could see him wringing his hands nervously in his lap. I put my hands behind my back. "It's okay to feel nervous but you shouldn't always show it to other people. Now if you put your hands under the table nobody would ever know and you would still look very powerful to everyone. I am nervous too, but can you tell?"

He thought on this for a little while. "Why are you nervous?"

"Because you are my only son and I love you so much, but I am afraid you will be scared of me."

Instead of removing his hands, he flattened them on the table. "I'm not nervous anymore so I don't need to hide them. I'm not afraid of scars. Charlotte has a scar too," he announced.

"Well then little Mr. King you're the most powerful man here."

"Show your scar, Charlotte," he said.

Charlotte turned her hand over and I saw the white scar on the inside of her wrist.

"You can touch it, Daddy," he said. "Go on, Daddy."

I reached my hand and let my finger trace the smooth scar. I could feel her blood pounding under my skin and my own blood heating up, the sweat on my skin starting to sizzle. I wanted to grasp her wrist, pull her to me, and kiss her right there, but I didn't even look up into her face. I lifted my hand and looked at my son.

He smiled suddenly, a big beaming smile, and it warmed my heart to bursting.

When I was slightly more composed I turned to Charlotte and caught the look in her eyes as she watched me. It was one of complete adoration. I felt almost lightheaded with joy. I couldn't take my eyes off her.

Fortunately, she had better sense than me. She turned away quickly. "See, Zackary," she said to him, "there's nothing to be afraid of. Your father is brilliant, is he not?"

For a moment Zackary looked like he wanted to disagree, and the genuine indecision on his face made Charlotte laugh. A second later, I forgot to be self-conscious that I was the butt of their joke and laughed too. Because he did truly look so adorable. I was fascinated by my son. He had grown so much. He could understand everything I said, and talk back. It was wonderful.

Carrie came from the house carrying a tray with little desserts on it. She asked if I wanted something to drink, but I refused. Charlotte immediately stood and started to do something with the tray. My eyes slid over to her. She was in a pair of tight jeans and I couldn't help but notice the curve of her hips. She had a beautiful full butt. The kind that you wanted to watch as she rode you reverse cowboy. I thought of it spread out on my stomach.

Suddenly, I was rock hard in the gazebo with my son a few feet away. It was the last thing I fucking needed. I quickly turned my attention back to my son. "So when do we fly the kite, then?"

"After dessert," Charlotte said, turning back to catch my gaze.

I didn't look away, and she couldn't have missed the raw desire for her that consumed me day and night.

She forced a smile to her face and held out a little plate. There was a dainty square piece of chocolate dessert on it. I stabbed it with my fork and pushed the whole thing into my mouth. Fuck, I was so turned on, it tasted of nothing. To my surprise, my son copied my action exactly.

With his mouth full, he announced, "I'm ready."

"Wait for Charlotte," I said, and we sat there and watched her eat her piece. She had no idea what she was doing to me. Or maybe she did. Hell, the woman ate chocolate as if she was giving it a blowjob.

I stood from the chair not knowing what to do. She finished her dessert and we walked to the middle of the green she said, "Aren't you going to show Daddy your painting?"

Immediately, Zackary held his kite up for me. I stopped walking and stared at the figure of a man with the black face. That stick figure was me. I was holding hands with another smaller stick figure. I looked from the painting to Zackary's face.

He took the kite from me. "That's you me and Mummy," he declared proudly, stabbing at the three stick figures.

I had to fight back tears. In his world, we were holding hands.

"Don't be rough with the kite," Charlotte cautioned softly.

Zackary became as still as a statue. His degree of concentration was amusing and I would have laughed out loud if my heart didn't feel as if it was in a vise.

Charlotte tapped affectionately on the tip of his nose. "You don't have to go that still."

I had never flown a kite. Until I was ten and before Stanley came into my life, my childhood consisted of schoolwork, housework, and regular beatings. Since I didn't know how to fly one, I sat back down when we made it to the middle of the green and watched them.

It was a windy day and they struggled with the kite, but every moment was one to be relished. I watched as they ran about on the grounds with the kite, crashing it continuously, until finally it rose into the air. For a time I held my breath and felt the beauty that could be found in the simplest of activities.

Until the kite got lost in a tree.

Both of them looked as though they would burst into tears and I couldn't tell who was the child.

"Go get the gardener, Zackary," she said.

He ran off and she came over to me. "Thank you, Brett, for taking the time for us."

"I should be thanking you," I said to her. And I really meant it. It had been the best hour of my life.

Zackary was racing over to us. "Brian is coming," he shouted excitedly.

"Let's head over to the tap to wash off these grass stains," she said to him.

At the tap, exactly what I expected happened. Charlotte sprayed Zackary with a blast from the hosepipe and I watched as they got into a little water fight. I would have been fully included, but neither was familiar with me as of yet, so I got off with a few stray blasts.

Our laughter rang out into the early afternoon skies, and it was a memory I knew I would never forget. Charlotte was soaked, her white blouse glued to her chest and giving me a perfect view of her breasts. I couldn't hold back any longer.

"Zackary, go and ask for some towels from Mrs. Blackmore," I instructed.

He hurried away obediently towards the kitchens.

I would have approached her, but it turned out she was the one in that moment who longed for me even more than I did her.

"Let's call a truce," she said. I felt the heat of her gaze. We were drenched, but I felt like my whole body was on fire. Her earlier rejection felt like a forgotten memory. The bulge of her nipples through the white cotton material hardened me even further, and more than anything I wanted to have them in my mouth.

"Will you take your mask off?" She took a step forward and to my surprise my feet took me backwards.

I could not believe I was retreating. She took another then but this time, I forced myself to hold still. Cowardice was not a word I acknowledged in anything that I did, and it wasn't going to start with her.

"You're the one who can't seem to look me in the eyes now," she said, and her tone was anything but smug. She looked terrified, and yet unable to control herself from coming forward.

Her hands were on my shoulders for support, and before I could work out her full intention her lips were on mine. She kissed me, her tongue softly nudging my lips apart. For a few seconds, I relished the taste that was solely hers.

Then I crushed my lips to hers.

My strength pushed her backwards so with my arm around her waist I cushioned the impact as her back connected with the old wall. My mouth feasted on her lips and then sucked on the plump bottom one. The kiss was desperate, and all-consuming.

Somewhere in the distance I heard Zackary call out to her, but I still couldn't pull away from her.

"Charlotte? Where are you?" his little voice rang out.

Eventually when his voice got too close, I found the will. I ended the kiss, and turning around, walked away. But it felt as if I was walking on air.

My whole world was shaken. Now I knew. I could not let Charlotte go.

CHAPTER 41

CHARLOTTE

I watched him go, my nails digging into my palms.

Zackary met him on the way, the towels in hand and for a moment he stopped, seemingly unsure of what to do without me there. He appeared even unable to look up at his father. Slowly, as if he was afraid to spook the boy, Brett lowered himself and silently held out his hand. I watched Zackary eventually find the courage to look him in the eye, and then shakily extend a towel out to him.

I could almost feel the smile underneath his mask as he accepted the towel from his son, patted it across his forehead, then rose to his feet again.

He turned around and shot me a glance. My hands were flattened against the stone wall to keep me stable, and I was still breathing hard. The look he gave me was searing. I just stared back at him. When he looked away and took his leave, I shut my eyes and prepared myself to be normal for Zackary.

Opening my eyes, I dropped to the ground, my arms spread

out for a hug. Zackary ran into them. In just a short time he had transformed into the sweetest child I'd ever known.

"Thank you," I whispered almost tearfully in his ear.

"You're welcome," he said handing me the towel.

He thought I was thanking him for the towel, but I was being grateful to him for not freaking out and for trying his very best to welcome his father.

We went back indoors and the rest of the day passed with lessons and his schedule of activities. When evening came upon us we went in for dinner; this time I allowed Zackary to have his meal with the rest of the staff. I had to admit I was nervous that at any moment his mother would return to meet the scene of her son sharing his meal with the servants and completely lose it.

But I didn't lose my nerve.

I opened a window, even though it had turned quite cold, and kept an ear open for the sounds of cars approaching. Instead of his carefully prepared, highly nutritious meals, I allowed him to eat the same food as us all. It wouldn't hurt just this once. Soon I would be gone and I wanted him to enjoy my last few days here.

It was one of the best meals we have ever had. Mr. Boothsworth produced a bottle of gooseberry gin his friend made at home. It was strong stuff and Mrs. Blackmore got drunk after one glass. It was funny to watch her. She started tickling Zackary and flirting openly with Mr. Boothsworth and it was finally clear to everybody that they had a thing going on in secret. It made me quite happy to see them like that.

Carrie and Bella were as merry as I'd ever seen them, and I laughed at the appalled expression on Zackary's face when they took turns in stealing bits of sausage from his toad in the hole.

The alcohol had gone to my head as well. Coupled with the magic of the day and the lovely floating feeling, I returned to my room emotionally and physically exhausted, but happy.

I found myself immediately going towards the window and standing by it, wishing his silhouette would appear. How long I remained there, hoping, I wasn't sure, but eventually thunder struck across the sky, and soon the cold, ferocious rain came pouring down. Just as I had given up the idea of seeing him, he appeared. This time I knew for certain that he was staring directly at me … watching me … craving me just as I was him.

I placed my hand on my chest to settle my erratic heart, wondering if responding to it and to him was the way to go. What good could possibly come out of this besides my heart being broken when it all came to an end?

He wanted me, but I was not deceived that it was anything more than just a sexual longing on his part. *What would it take to fuck you?* No, I wasn't deceived as to what our positions in the world were. I was only a nanny, to Jillian, I was even her servant, while he held the baton of wealth and prestige.

Maybe that was my shield of goodness. The impossibility of us ever being together meant I wouldn't give in to the raging lust in my body. It was my default to always give a hundred percent, but 100 percent would not be needed this time. All there would be is time to just revel in it and tuck away the memories of whatever moments I could find in his arms.

Memories to be taken out and relived when I was old.

I shivered from the chill and turned away to head down the stairs. I was suddenly thirsty and cold. During weather like this my mother always used to brew us both a cup of tea. I decided I would do that. I was halfway down the stairs when I realized I had not brought my baby monitor, but I knew he was sleeping deeply and I would only be a few minutes.

Sure enough less than ten minutes later I had the steaming mug in hand and I was making my way across the dimly lit house when a sudden scream shook the house. I almost let go of the mug as my heart jumped into my throat. It was Zackary, there was no mistaking it. Before I could even start running towards him, I heard the thudding sound of a body rolling and tumbling. The mug fell from my hands and crashed on the stone floor as I started running towards the stairs. To my horror, I saw Zackary's white little body falling down the stairs, hitting every hard step, in a dead silence. I almost passed out in fear.

"Zackary," I screamed, and raced towards him.

He lay sprawled at the bottom, motionless, face down. No, no, no. I was so frightened my knees felt like jelly as I fell to my haunches next to him.

"Zackary," I called, my entire being stricken with panic.

I turned him around. He was breathing, but his eyes were closed and a blue bruise was already forming on his fore-head. But even worse his mouth was full of blood. Red blood seeped out of his mouth, scaring the shit out of me.

Without moving him, I ran back up the stairs to grab my phone. The tears were rolling down from my eyes as I dialed

999. I managed to make myself understood and requested an ambulance. Then I hit the intercom and screamed for anybody at all to come to the bottom of the stairs.

Mrs. Blackmore was the closest and she was the first to arrive. Her hair was in blue rollers and she was wearing a long white nightgown. "What happened?" she cried, her face pale without her make-up.

Before I could answer, Mr. Boothsworth came hurrying in. He had drunk too much at dinner and he looked a bit confused. Then from the top of the stairs Brett appeared.

"What the fuck?" he exploded as he ran down the stairs and knelt beside his son's still body.

"I've called the ambulance," I said, my voice shaking. I tried my best not to cry as I stared at the helpless child. I felt so guilty. If I had taken the baby monitor I would have heard him calling out. I shouldn't have had that drink. I was supposed to be working.

Mr. Boothsworth positioned himself next to Brett. "I used to work in a hospital. Let me," he offered urgently.

Immediately Brett moved to make space for him and Mr. Boothsworth moved his hands quickly over Zackary's small body. "It doesn't look like any of his bones are broken and his breathing is even so for now things are stable. I think we'll risk it and take him to ER ourselves."

"Get a blanket," Brett barked, and Mrs. Blackmore and I both started to run up the stairs, but she held out her hand to me to indicate that she would get it. Brett telephoned someone and ordered him to start the helicopter. He then called someone named Logan to prepare for the helicopter to land close to the hospital that was an hour's drive away and have a car ready to pick him up.

"Can I please come?" I begged.

Brett nodded grimly, then he carefully lifted Zackary into his arms. Mr. Boothsworth opened the back door and Brett walked out into the night with his precious cargo and me following, with my heart in my mouth.

While we were on our way to the landing pad Zackary started moaning. I was so happy to hear him conscious I started crying with joy. Gently, very gently, Brett spoke to him and stroked his hair. "It's okay, Zackary. I'm here. You're safe. Nothing bad can happen to you."

"Daddy?"

"Yes, it's Daddy."

"My head hurts, Daddy."

"I know, darling. It's just a temporary thing. We're going to the hospital now and the doctors will make it all better. You have to be brave, okay?"

"What happened?"

"You fell down the stairs."

"I did?"

Then he lost consciousness again and Brett stared ahead. I knew he was willing the journey to be over soon. His jaw was clenched so tight his skin, already so pale, looked bone white. For the rest of the journey I prayed, God how I prayed, that all would be well.

Soon we were getting into a waiting vehicle and before long we arrived at the hospital. Staff took Zackary from us, put him on a gurney, and wheeled him away. I wanted to bawl my eyes out. Wordlessly his father drew me into his arms, and I held onto the front of his shirt in desperation. I loved that little boy so much, even the thought of him being hurt was unbearable.

It seemed forever before the doctor returned. "You said he fell down a flight of stairs?"

I nodded frantically.

"It seems he has a concussion."

"What about the blood in his mouth," I asked anxiously.

"It looks like he just knocked a tooth loose, but we will find out more after some tests. Please calm down and wait patiently. The good news is he is currently not in much danger."

The relief I felt drained the strength from my legs and I would have sunk to the floor if Brett had not caught me and helped me to a chair.

In time we were ushered to Zackary's room. The lights were switched off and he was hooked up to equipment that bleeped and emitted a pale green glow. Neither Brett nor I tried to speak. We just sat there in complete silence. I stared down at the frail child and just prayed that no lasting damage had been done.

After a while, Brett pulled my hand and we both exited the room. Outside, in the corridor it seemed too bright.

"It's my fault," I whispered.

"Don't be silly. Accidents happen, it's not your fault. He was probably just scared by the rain and wanted to find you."

"I should have taken the baby monitor with me," I cried.

"Come on. How were you to know? It won't help him at all if you beat yourself up over this. I'll call a car for you. Go back and get some rest. I'll hang around here and make sure his test results are fine."

"I'll stay," I said. "I won't be able to sleep anyway. Besides if he wakes up, I want him to see a familiar face." And then I realized what I said, and quickly added. "I'm sorry I didn't mean it like that."

But he shook his head dismissively. "It's not important. Don't give it another thought."

"We can take turns," I said.

"Yes," he said softly, and rubbing the back of his neck looked around him. "I can't wait to take him back. As you can imagine I have quite the distaste for hospitals."

CHAPTER 42

CHARLOTTE

"The same goes for me," I said.

He turned to look at me. "Why is that?"

"I had a friend who had acid thrown on her face by her ex. He swore if he couldn't have her, no one would. So he had the great idea of splashing her face with acid. She lost an eye and her pain was so intense she was unable to even shut her eyes for a moment to sleep. She was a very beautiful girl and she couldn't take it to see what she had become. I'd go to see her in hospital every day and she would say nothing. I knew she was awake, but she was unwilling to move, or speak, or acknowledge anyone at all. In the end she took her own life. And then my father went and died in one. So, you see, hospitals are not my favorite place either."

"I'm sorry," he said, his gaze boring into mine.

I knew he was thinking about his own disfigurement.

"Do you want something to drink?" he asked suddenly.

I nodded and watched him leave. He was in a camel coat that

went past his calves. Mrs. Blackmore had chosen it and brought it to him because it was just the right thickness for the weather, and he had carelessly thrown it over his shoulder, but it perfectly complemented the plain white shirt he had tucked into his dark gray slacks.

The ensemble, although simple would have made anyone look regal, but coupled with the natural grace of his frame, and the layer of mystery and danger that the mask added to his demeanor, he almost looked too intimidating to approach.

He returned a few minutes later with a bottle of juice and water. I chose the juice and lifted it to my lips while he kept the water by his side.

"Aren't you going to drink something?" I asked.

"Later," he replied, his gaze ahead and deep in thought.

It was late at night and we were the only ones in that waiting room. "Who do you wear the mask for? Yourself or others?"

He didn't look away. "I wear it for myself because of others."

"Because they'll pity you?"

"Because they'll make me angry. I don't want any eyes on me …" He turned away. "I never did."

"What about my eyes?" I asked.

For the longest time, he watched me without moving, until I lifted my hands. The moment I touched the sides of his face, he lowered his head. I went on, towards his ears, carefully, but when I touched the string to pull it away, he caught my wrist.

His touch seared me and I waited with bated breath. For what exactly, I was unsure.

"Your pulse is racing," he murmured.

I said the first thought that came to mind. "I want to see you."

He smiled, sadly, and roved his eyes over my face, his gaze settling on my lips. "And I want to fuck you."

In that moment … the world, time … and my breathing slowed down. My heart stuttered in response, and it made me breathless. "Okay."

His eyes widened.

I returned my gaze to his hold on my wrist, and began to reach again for the string around his ear.

"Charlotte …" he warned, but I ignored him, overtaken by determination.

"I want to look at you … please … let me."

CHAPTER 43

BRETT

https://www.youtube.com/watch?v=pHuDGv53dcA
Good Girls Go To Heaven (Bad Girls Go Everywhere)

She was unraveling me, and I hated it.

I was terrified … but at the same time I craved it. Sparks of excitement electrified my brain.

I knew that she wouldn't reject me, but I didn't want her to know just how ugly I was. The way the nurses, the doctors, Jillian, the orderly who came into my room, my son reacted. Those memories told me she was going to get a shock. That somehow she had built it up in her mind that I had a few white scars like the one she had on her wrist.

Then I looked into her eyes and suddenly, I knew I wanted her to see.

If she showed disgust I would know then that it was over. I didn't need to masturbate to fantasies of her every night, twice. I could forget her. Stop hoping and just go back to life as it was before she breezed into my life.

My hold began to loosen around her wrist as she began to pull the string away.

We were the only ones seated in the corridor, and although it was softly lit, the light was enough for her to have her fill. The mask came away in her hand, and I was revealed in all my hideousness. The scars, the skinless bits, the brutally mangled flesh. I didn't dare meet her gaze, but as she traced her fingers over it as if in awe, my body trembled.

"It was hell, wasn't it?" she asked.

Tears filled my eyes.

When she brought her forehead to mine and then placed a kiss against it, the tears rolled down my cheeks. I closed my eyes when she began to trail kisses down my nose. But when she placed her lips on my scars I couldn't take it anymore. I tried to pull away, but she grabbed hold of my head.

My eyes shot open then and I met her tear-soaked face.

"I don't want you to pity me," I said, a bite in my tone I had not intended.

Her snort was incredulous. She wiped her eyes with the back of her sleeves. "It's not pity. I'm just angry, that you had to go through all of this without me by your side."

My eyes widened in shock.

She couldn't be real ...

That was all I could think, but in that moment I didn't want her to be. I wanted to believe that she was this angel that I could love and she would love me back and we would live together happily ever after. I could feel my control of the situation and myself slipping, and it was too much to handle. It was real.

I pulled her hand away and rose to my feet.

"I'm going to get some coffee," I said. "You should go back. I'll call Logan and get him to come pick you up."

She rose with me. "I don't want you to leave."

It sounded like a fucking order. I turned around to stare at her. "What did you say?"

"You wanted to fuck me, didn't you?" she asked.

I stared at her. Under normal circumstances no one in their right mind would want to have sex in a hospital, with sex and death for company, especially when their son is lying in one of the rooms, but nothing about this moment was normal. The stress of rushing Zackary to hospital, not knowing if he had forever damaged his spine or damaged his brain, then the joy of knowing he would be fine, combined with the intense sexual desire we had built up had screwed me over.

I couldn't even think rationally anymore.

"Well, what are you waiting for?" She brushed her hair away from her shoulder and began to walk away. For a second I was frozen. I couldn't believe it. Then I followed her, until we reached an empty room where they stored brushes and brooms.

She went in.

The moment I joined her she jammed the door shut. My cock was already painfully hard as she slipped her sweater down her arms and pulled up her night dress. She pushed me down on a metal table and sat astride me. With her gaze locked on mine she pulled away the mask that I was holding tightly in my hand.

She tossed it to the floor, and with my face in her hands, crushed her lips to mine. Her kiss was ferocious, her tongue plunging into my mouth and warning me of the urgency of her lust.

I sat back as she ravaged me, my hands sliding up her warm skin until they arrived at her breasts. She was braless. In all the worry and tension about Zackary I had not noticed. Her nipples hardened and strained against my hand as I closed them around the full, soft mounds, kneading and pumping.

She began to grind against me, her clit pressed to the bulge of my swollen cock. I felt it all for the gorgeous woman astride me … lust … warmth … possession … pride. She was going to make me lose my mind. Dragging my lips from hers, I threw my arms around her pressing my head to her chest as I tried to catch my breath.

She stilled for a moment and then threw her arms around my head. Our passion rose and built as she ground her open pussy against my cock. Unable to take anymore, my hands shot to the waistband of my slacks. I began to jerk it open. In no time, my cock sprang free. Instantly, her hands closed around it with delicious excitement. I buried my head underneath her dress and drew her breast into my mouth.

While I sucked her nipple, she stroked me, her fingers circling the broad tip, then running down the length. When she cupped my heavy balls, she breathed into my ear, "My, my, Mr. King, what a monster you have hidden away in your pants."

The compliment brought a ray of sunshine into my heart. It had been so long since a woman wanted me. Or thought I was attractive. She began to pull away, but my teeth wouldn't let go of her nipple.

"Ouch," she complained.

Before I could stop her she had sank down to her knees and covered my slick head with her mouth.

I spread my legs apart, unbridled lust taking over, lost, slamming my groin into her wet mouth. And she, she sucked fervently on my cock, her teeth deliberately scraping, making me shudder as she moved up and down my length.

Needing to hold onto my sanity, my hands gripped her hair as her mouth hollowed to take as much of my cock as would go down her throat. She was delicious. There was no other word to describe her. I felt like the luckiest man on earth. My head fell backward and an animalistic groan of sheer pleasure tore from deep inside me.

I looked down and my whole dick was deep in her hot, slick throat, but it was not enough.

I needed my penis inside her. Inside that pretty pink cunt just as I had imagined countless times lying alone in my bed. With my hands under her arms I lifted her up, my cock slipping out of her mouth with a plop.

"I need to be inside you," I said. I had no condom. But it didn't matter. Condoms are for people who have something to lose. People who are afraid of diseases and unwanted pregnancies. I wanted anything and everything this woman could give me. I could handle disease, and I desperately wanted her babies. I wanted a football pitch full of children from this woman's womb.

I tore away her panties and flung the scrap of material from us. The wetness of her pussy rubbed against my dick. Her hand gripped my shoulders for support. She rode the hardened length, breathless and with a dirty smile across her face that I relished.

She rose suddenly to her feet, and for a moment I was disoriented, almost close to panic. Then she lifted one leg up and slammed her swollen wet pussy on my face. My fingers dug into her luscious ass, as my mouth began to eat up her pussy.

Her moan was belly deep and sent shivers down my spine.

She was fucking delicious.

My hands held her hips in place as she ground her pussy against my tongue. I nipped at her clit and licked her slit cleanly through. Then I rounded my lips and sucked eagerly on the protruding bud of her sex.

"*Fuck*," she cursed and I swore right then that it was the most beautiful word in the English language.

She came all over my face, her hands in my hair as she bucked, her hips fucking my mouth with wild abandon.

I couldn't breathe and for the moment didn't need to. I would have gladly suffocated to death beneath her and as she pulled away to gaze at me, the conclusion clear in my eyes as I struggled to catch my breath, she burst into laughter.

"I'm sorry … Sir," she said. "I got a bit carried away."

With my gaze on hers, and my heart brimming with pure joy, I guided her hips back to mine.

"I hate it when you apologize for no reason," I said.

"Your face is covered in my juices, Sir," she said cheekily, and began to lick me off. She cleaned her cum off my scars and I crushed her tightly to me, feeling the kind of love I couldn't believe was possible. When she was done, she slipped her tongue into my mouth and I relished that naughty pink tease as it did its best to provoke me.

I couldn't wait any longer.

Grabbing her hips I guided her over my cock. With a saucy smile she pushed her pussy against my cock and bounced her slick slit up and down the shaft.

"This bad boy and I are going to become best friends," she said.

That was the best proposal I had ever had. No negotiation required. I stilled her hips, and with my gaze locked on hers, slammed her down on my cock.

"*Accepted.*" I grunted.

"Fuuuuuuuuck," came her agonizing cry. It was long and bone deep, as her cunt swallowed my cock greedily. Just as I had imagined.

Then holding my gaze, she lifted herself up slowly. At the tip she paused, and I could feel her juices dripping down my shaft.

"My God," she cried to the ceiling. Head thrown back, she slammed back down again. This time all the way down. Right to the fucking root.

With my face buried in her breasts, I dug my fingers into her luxurious buttocks and guided her as U slid in and out of her.

"Charlotte," I rasped. I knew I wasn't making sense, but I needed to somehow convey what she was doing to me.

I thrust my hips violently upwards to meet her slams, until she began to ride even faster and with more rhythm than I could guide. I let my hands fall to the side and gave total control over to her to fuck me.

"*Fuck, fuck, fuck, fuck,*" she rasped.

Her cries were the sweetest of music to my ears. I'd always suspected it would be this way with her, but my God, my entire being was blown into incoherence.

She milked my shaft for all it was worth, writhing and rocking, riding and plunging. At her tight clench around me, her nails dug into my back, and I was sure I was going to find a trail of wounds down my flesh the following morning. I couldn't recall when I had looked forward to something more.

My orgasm built and built, but I held on, forcing myself to resist, until I could feel her about to explode all over me. Then, I reached into her crotch and rubbed her little clit, and she came with a scream, shaking violently, as her pussy rippled, convulsed, and contracted on my dick.

She was frozen with sensation, but I didn't stop.

I powered into her, driving relentlessly. When I came, my whole body jerked at the impact as hot seed spurted thickly into her.

I roared at the wonder, my hand gripping her neck, as my head fell against her.

"*Fuck*," I panted, energized with raw ecstasy. "*Fuuuuuck!*"

I could hear her laugh at my growls of awe at the intensity of my climax. The orgasm reverberated through me in waves and waves until I stopped falling, my entire being spent beyond comprehension.

"That was a long time coming," she muttered into my ear, and somehow I managed a laugh at the fully intended pun.

CHAPTER 44

We returned home with Zackary before the day broke.

Brett carried him, bundled in his blanket, up to his room while I followed. It made me quite happy when he woke up as he was laid down. His eyes were hazy as he tried to adjust to the light from his bedside lamp, his gaze moved from his father to me. He looked pitifully confused and my heart went out to him.

"Hey," I said and tapped the tip of his nose.

"Where am I?" he asked groggily.

"You are home, in your bedroom," Brett said.

"Oh." He yawned tiredly. "My head hurts," he muttered, lifting his hand to his head.

I caught the hand and pulled it back down to his side, and the poor thing winced at the pain in his arm. Even that little thing had hurt him. I wanted to cry then. I couldn't say a word, but I reminded myself of what the doctor said. He was going to be fine. No lasting damage had been done.

"Go back to sleep and get some rest, okay," his father said quietly.

"I don't feel sleepy. Can Charlotte read *Ali Baba And The Forty Thieves* for me?"

I was ready to set myself on fire if he had requested it, but I had a better idea. "I have to run to the bathroom now, but," I pulled out the book from the shelf above his bed, opened it at the bookmark, and thrust it into Brett's hand, "Daddy will read it for you. I'll be right back so start without me."

Brett raised his eyebrows at me, but I motioned to him to take over. Looking mighty uncomfortable he turned back to his son.

Both males looked lost as I began to walk away, but I pretended not to notice. I disappeared from the room, but left the door open just a crack wide so I could watch them.

I watched as Brett started from where I had stopped and began to read the story to Zackary. With a smile I went back to my room. Both April and my mother had called while I was at the hospital so I quickly sent them both a message that I would call them later in the morning. Then I collapsed on my bed and stared up at the ceiling.

Boy! What a night.

I held a hand to my poor heart. From the fright of a lifetime, I had been ushered into the fuck of the century, all within the space of six hours. I couldn't help the cat-got-the-cream smile that spread on my lips. I thought about what we had done, and the stirrings of arousal ignited and began to ripple through my body once again. It all was still so very vivid, the reminder of how I had been fucked to complete incoherence just a few hours ago.

And we didn't use a condom.

Even more surprising, I hadn't wanted one.

And I was the safe one. The one who warned everybody about STDs from one-night stands.

I knew I should get the morning after pill, but I didn't even want to do that. If I got pregnant from one perfect mating with Brett, then I wanted to keep that precious life. I wanted it more than I wanted anything else. Brett's baby. My baby. Nobody would understand, but I didn't care. I touched my stomach and prayed I had become pregnant.

Please God.

Then my thoughts moved on and I began to relive what we'd done in one of the most unromantic places in the world. Broom cupboards would never be the same again. My clit began to throb as I recalled the feel of Brett's cock in my mouth, and of his wild thrusts as he plunged in and out of me. I needed more. Before the sun fully rose and we all returned to reality. So I got up and opened my door wide to ensure that I did not miss Brett when he left Zackary's room. Fifteen minutes later he appeared at my door.

"Is he asleep?"

He nodded.

I opened my arms.

"Not here," he whispered, and he slipped his hands under me and scooped me up into his arms.

"I'm too heavy," I protested.

"No, you're not. You're as light as a feather."

"Wait," I said, and grabbed the baby monitor.

He carried me to his quarters and laid me down on his bed. I reached out my hand and pulled his mask away.

"I want to see your beautiful face," I said.

He kneeled on the floor in front of me. I was already so wet, but I felt myself gush when he said, "Show me your pussy, Miss Conrad, because I am hungry for her."

CHAPTER 45

CHARLOTTE

https://www.youtube.com/watch?v=dEWuAcMWDLY
You make me feel like a natural woman

I sneaked back to my room at dawn. It seemed like only a few minutes had passed before my alarm went off. I shot up from the bed, almost panicked. It was already seven o'clock. I hurried over to Zackary's room. I saw him still soundly asleep on his bed, but when I walked to his bed I saw the bruise on his forehead had already become purple. Thank God, he was breathing evenly.

Closing the door quietly, I headed down the stairs and met Mrs. Blackmore alone in the kitchen, sitting quietly and having a cup of tea. When she saw me she nodded. "I checked in on the little one earlier. He was sleeping like an angel, but that's some shiner he has on his forehead."

"Yeah, poor kid must be full of bruises."

"Mr. Boothsworth told me. Thank God it was nothing more serious. I can't imagine what this morning would be like if …" She shuddered. "Did you have a good rest, dear?"

I nodded, noting the ache that ran down my thighs as I sat down, but of course that had little to nothing to do with Zackary.

She rose then, wiping her hands on her apron. "I'll get you something to eat. It was a tough night was it not?"

"It was alright. Where is everyone?" I asked noting the unusually empty kitchen.

"Off to their chores … With what happened to Zackary we're expecting Madam back very soon so no one wants to be caught slacking off."

I felt a cold claw squeeze at my insides, but I tried to keep my gaze as neutral as possible. "Has someone told her then?"

"I would imagine Mr. King would. She is the boy's mother, after all."

I nodded.

She glanced at her watch. "He'll be leaving in an hour so I should start getting his meal ready now."

"I'll take it to him," I said to her. "I want to ask him some information about the hospital last night so I'll just take it to him when you're ready."

"Thank you, dear," she said with a grateful smile.

A quarter of an hour later I was at his door. As I brought up my hand to knock, I found it trembling. Taking a deep breath, I knocked, and when he didn't respond, I made my way in.

"Brett?" I called.

Placing his meal down, and getting no response, I headed into his bedroom to find it empty. From the sound of the running water I guessed he was in the bathroom, so I headed into the massive space.

The glass of his shower stall was frosty, but I could still see the outline of his frame as he stood gloriously tall and broad under the cascade, his palm was pressed against the wall and his gaze on the ground. He looked beautiful. Like the standing version of The Thinker statue pondering on some important matter.

For a second I hesitated interrupting him. Then, gearing up courage, I knocked softly on the glass door, and watched as he whirled his head around, water droplets flying away from him. He pulled the door opened and stood before me, gloriously naked, his cock bobbing slightly under its own weight.

I couldn't take my eyes off how glorious he was, until his greeting lifted my gaze to his.

"Enjoying the view?" he drawled.

I grinned. "Yes."

"I thought you would wake me up."

"I thought about it," I replied, "but you looked too peaceful asleep. I couldn't dare disrupt that."

"Alright," he said with a smile, "but don't do it again."

"Uh, I brought your meal. I've placed it on the table." I turned around and pretended to leave when he reached out and caught me before I could get away. I smiled as my body connected with his wet muscles. I could feel his cock hardening as it pressed against my buttocks. I thought of Mrs. King coming. This was her husband and her son I was playing house with. Then I thought about how little she cared for either one of them and I shut my eyes. The tug of arousal was almost unbearable as he slid his arms across my breasts.

He placed a hard kiss to the pulse in my neck and whispered in my ear, his hot breath tickling me. "Where do you think you're going, little Charlotte?"

Pulling up my dress to reveal my bare buttocks, I twirled it against his groin. "I have to … er … get Zackary up for the day."

"You had … er … a long night… you're allowed to sleep in."

I turned around and stared into his beautiful eyes. I love a man when his eyelashes are all wet and stuck together. "Don't you really mean to say that I'm allowed to fuck in, because I'm already wide awake?"

He was amused, but only for a fraction of a moment, then he looked away. My full focus on him had made him uncomfortable. He tilted his body to the right. Raising my hand, I placed it on the mottled, scarred part of his face and turned his gaze back to mine.

"You're not allowed to hide from me any longer," I said and crushed my lips to his.

I wasn't sure if he was the one who staggered at the contact, or if it was me … but his hold tightened around me to maintain our balance. My free hand slid across his ass to pull his hips closer still. I slipped my other hand around his neck and plunged my tongue as far down his mouth as it would go.

His hands pinched my nipples, the pressure pulling at the delicious strings of lust throughout my body. My body trembled as his hand slid down my front to palm my mound, his fingers slipping towards my creamy pussy. I gasped aloud as he slipped two fingers inside of me.

His thrusts sent both of my hands around his neck, my hips riding and thrusting against the assault. To my great surprise, I climaxed almost immediately. My groan was breathless as I came against his fingers … my juices spilling out and running down his hand. It was a wildly arousing sight especially when he brought his hand to his mouth and licked it clean.

I slipped out of my dress and threw it on the dry floor outside the shower. With both hands on his chest, I pushed him gently back into the stall, so he was now under the cascade of water. My clit was still throbbing painfully between my legs. I wanted him where I could bury his face properly into my pussy and do that thing he did so well. I needed him to soothe the maddening, insatiable ache.

There were so many things I wanted to do to him, so many ways that I wanted to touch him, and be touched in this stall, that I didn't even know where to begin. I wanted his dick filling me up until I thought I would explode, stretching my walls, and reveling in the waves of pleasure that would wreak through my body, but at the same time I wanted to come instantly again and to feel the hot spurt of his semen inside me.

His eyes bored into me as he slanted his lips over mine. The water cascaded down on us, my rock-hard nipples were crushed against his chest. Grabbing his penis, I fisted the thick, rock hard length with both of my hands before sliding it up and down my soaked sex.

He spun me back to face the tile wall. With his hands around my thighs, he jutted out my hips, spreading my ass completely open for him.

"Brett," I called out helplessly.

He leaned over to whisper into my ear. "I love the way you call me …"

"Brett," I called again, my voice the most sultry I had ever heard it.

Bending his knees, he aligned himself to me and circled my opening with the head of his shaft.

I shut my eyes, my head thrown backwards as I anticipated his plunge into me. No one had gone deeper than he had. I waited, my teeth biting down painfully on my lips, but he took his time, delaying his complete possession until I was close to being driven mad.

"Brett," I rasped out loud, my hips writhing with anticipation and encouragement.

"Tell me you want me," he ordered, nipping the shell of my ear, while his fingers flicked my painfully sensitive clit.

"I want you," I said. "I want you right now, Brett. More than anything else …" I could barely catch my breath. "Please … please, fuck me. Fuck me out of my mind."

"That's good enough for me," he muttered, just before he grabbed my hips in his big hands and slammed into me so violently my legs left the floor.

I slapped my hands against the wet wall, again and again, needing to tear or break something with the wild sensations that were coursing through me. My grunt was nothing short of animalistic. Every sense in me became alive and electrified, the feel of his cock inside me, the taste of the water pouring into my mouth, the sound of his breathing, and the touch of his body surrounding me, inside me. It was euphoric.

He drove into me mercilessly.

My responses to his thrusts were completely feral. Just the instinct of a woman being taken by a man. I writhed, and jerked and twerked my hips against his.

Ferocious ecstasy tore through me. With his hand on the small of my back he bent me even lower. I clenched my eyes shut and let him pound into me.

His hands were digging into the side of my hips, and his balls slamming against the curve of my buttocks. "*Charlotte,*" he roared out. "Oh fuck … *Fuck.*"

More than anything I was loving the fact that I was able to do this for him.

"How can you feel this fucking good?" he growled. "My God, I'm gone …"

And he was.

I freed one hand and circled my clitoris with ferocious strokes. He slammed into me one last time and we both exploded, a scream tearing from my mouth.

With his face buried in my neck, he pumped into me, wrenching every last ounce of uncontainable lust out of our bodies. I felt floaty and lightheaded. From somewhere seemingly far, but still close to me, I heard the grunts from deep within his throat and my labored breathing.

"Brett," I cried, tears rolling down my face.

He held me desperately to him. "You were made for me," he swore. "No one else. You're mine, Charlotte Conrad. I swear it you're mine. And one day you'll carry my name too."

I loved his words, relishing them and holding them close to my heart. "I'm yours," I sobbed, even though I was almost too scared to believe him. In that moment reality was too far away to disturb either of us. We clung on to each other, desperately, our bodies stuck to each other with the mind-blowing realization that we were both as close to love as either of us had ever come in our lives.

Mrs. King was far from our minds.

CHAPTER 46

BRETT

The next day I was invited to dinner with Charlotte and Zackary. I looked at the childish writing on the formal card and smiled.

They were waiting by the front door when I arrived home the next day, and I wondered what the reception was for, but at the welcoming smile on Charlotte's face I felt my insides warm with love for her. Zackary had his hands in hers, and for a moment I felt a slight pang of unwarranted jealousy toward my son.

Then the feeling was gone. They were the two angels in my life.

I got out of the car and Charlotte sent Zackary forward. I watched as the little man approached. "I would like to extend an invitation to join me and Charlotte for dinner," he said, and for a moment I thought that my heart would burst. No longer was he cowering away or reluctant to even look me in the eye. I didn't even correct the me and Charlotte mistake he made.

Lowering myself so we could be at eye level with each other, I looked into his eyes, and smiled gently.

"I'd love to have dinner with Charlotte and you."

His grin was infectious.

I straightened and looked at Charlotte. Mr. Boothsworth stood a short distance away from her, but I didn't pay him any mind. I stared intently at her, wanting my gaze to convey my gratitude for the way she was turning the light back on in the various aspects of my life.

I strolled down to the main dining room with Zackary and Charlotte, and soon we were seated at the grand table. Not once had I eaten at the table before this.

I noted my meal for the first time in as long as I could remember.

Charlotte sat beside me, and more times than I could count my gaze would slide to her ... roving over her face. I drowned in the blue pools of her eyes. The night was perfect, punctuated by laughs, and the twinkle in her eyes as she expertly handled my son. I could have lived that dinner again and again for the rest of my life. The most wonderful Groundhog's Day scenario.

She was a joy, through and through, and the moment Zackary agreed to run the errand of asking for our dessert, I lifted my hand from her lap and began to trace little circles up and down her arms.

"I'm enjoying my time with Zackary," I said to her. "But I need to be inside you. All day at work I couldn't think straight. I won't be able to manage myself for much longer."

She turned pink as she tried hard to brush off my hand. She looked nervously around to be sure that we didn't have an audience. "You need to give your full concentration to Zackary right now," she said to me. "It's rare that you have time to spend with him in this way. Since you both finally have a chance to develop a bond ..."

At the sound of voices beyond, she turned to see who was approaching, and I took advantage of her distraction. The moment she turned back I captured her lips in mine.

Her moan was instant. And the shot of pleasure to my groin was unmistakable. I shifted uncomfortably at the stiffening of my cock. My hand slid into her skirt just before the sound of heavy footsteps approached. I pulled away from her and couldn't help smiling at her. There were stars in her eyes and just like me she couldn't look away.

Until Mr. Boothsworth cleared his throat.

I turned at the interruption.

There was a strange expression on his face. "Madam is here," he announced, just before my wife appeared at the entrance to the dining room. She was dressed unusually casually in a pair of jeans and a green top, but she killed the effect by loading up on jewelry.

For the longest time she stared at the both of us and I boldly held her gaze. I was annoyed to say the least. I had told her to finish her rehab course. There was no need to return, but of course, she had to immediately disregard any sane advice.

Charlotte instantly began to rise from her chair, but I shot out an arm and placed it on hers. She sat back down.

Jillian stared at my hold on Charlotte's arm with an incredulous gaze. She didn't say a word, and only turned when Zackary and Mrs. Blackmore came into the room with the dessert. He was as careful with the little cake as he was with everything else, but when he realized his mother was there he immediately stood to attention. The smile was wiped from his face and he stared up at his mother as if he was uncertain whether he should go to her.

"Madam." Mrs. Blackmore bowed in greeting.

Jillian turned her gaze to Zackary.

"Mummy," he eventually called out.

"Come to me," she ordered in a shrill voice.

Mrs. Blackmore relieved the plate from the boy and he ran to his mother and hugged her legs, but it was an unnatural gesture. She turned to look at Charlotte, her mouth tightening again. "Why are you not wearing your glasses?"

"I don't wear them all the time," Charlotte replied.

Slowly, Jillian roved her gaze around the room, and then finally settled it on me. "What's going on?" she asked. "What are you doing here?"

My response was simple. "This is my house." And it held the answers to all her questions.

I saw the realization dawn in her eyes, and almost smiled with satisfaction. Finally, she knew what it felt like to watch the other person bring their lover to the house. She patted Zackary's head, and turning around walked away without another word.

CHAPTER 47

Over the next two days, I tried my very best to steer clear of Jillian, however the same courtesy was not extended back to me.

Before her return, I could count the number of times I personally had any interactions with her, but in the wake of her return she made it her goal to be more present and involved in every aspect of the household's affairs.

With exception of Mr. Boothsworth, who seemed to be particularly unaffected by Mrs. King's obtrusive presence, the rest of the staff seemed to be on high alert as we tiptoed about with our duties.

I was overseeing the packaging of a picnic lunch for Mrs. King and Zackary to take on an afternoon away, when Bella and Carrie walked into the kitchen.

Mrs. Blackmore and I both lifted our heads from the tarts and fruit we were packing. Carrie came over to the tray of flapjacks sitting in the middle of the table. She pulled out a chair quietly and almost whispered to Mrs. Blackmore. "Can I have one of these?"

Mr. Boothsworth plopped his empty mug of tea on the desk. The jarring sound made us all jump and we gave him a questioning look.

"What is happening?" he asked, his voice unusually loud, or maybe we were all just unusually quiet, we couldn't tell anymore.

"What do you mean?" Mrs. Blackmore responded.

"The entire household seems to be walking on egg shells. Am I missing something?"

"Lower your voice," Mrs. Blackmore muttered.

He frowned in confusion. "Why?"

"Mrs. King has been strange since she returned and it gives me the hebe jeebies."

"How so?" Mr. Boothsworth asked, not as familiar with the intricacies of women's ways.

"She doesn't go out as much anymore," Mrs. Blackmore answered, "and she seems unusually quiet. It's like the calm before the storm."

"Not quiet," Carrie corrected, "Watchful. I swear I feel as though I'm about to get fired at any moment."

"Me too," Bella added from her stance by the refrigerator as she drank some fruit infused water. "What surprises me the most is how much time she is now spending with Zackary. She put him to bed last night, Charlotte, did she not? And now today they're heading out for the afternoon, picnic basket and all. I've worked here for two years and this has never happened. The woman hates the outdoors. She brought the house down because of a spider in her room."

"She's also been lurking around a lot near the Master's wing. I don't know what she's doing there," Mrs. Blackmore added with a sigh. "The last time I nearly died of fright when I went in there to check on the towels and she was behind the door. I swear I feel like I'm going to pass out from all the tension. Thank God, Mr. King has gone away for a few days to France, or my poor nerves will never be able to settle down."

"Charlotte what about you?" Mr. Boothsworth called when I remained silent. "Do you also think Madam is behaving strangely?"

I didn't know what to say. Brett wanted to take me with him to France, but I knew it was the wrong time. I didn't want to give her a chance to poison the boy so I stayed, but I almost wish I had gone. Especially now with everyone looking at me for an answer. Luckily for me, Carrie saved me from having to answer that loaded question.

"Charlotte seems to be the luckiest," Carrie said. "By spending so much time with Zackary, Madam has cut her workload in half, while the rest of us are using a magnifying glass to polish the floors." She turned to me and pouted to show that she did not mean the rest of her words. "I envy you."

"I don't think so," Bella refuted. "Somehow I feel as though this is all hugely centered around Charlotte. I haven't actually seen her speak to Charlotte since she returned. She's been passing out instructions through everyone else. Do you think that she is upset because you somehow got Zackary close to his father again?"

"That is true," Mrs. Blackmore said slowly. "All this started when she came back and found him at dinner with Zackary and Charlotte."

Everybody turned to look at me and I could feel the color burn up my throat until the shrill of the intercom rang right then through the room. Everyone jumped, especially me. At first no one moved, then Mr. Boothsworth muttered, "Talk of the devil," and got up to answer it. We all listened to her cold voice come through. When the call ended, he turned to us. We all stared at each other, some of us, not me, had silent fright in our eyes.

"You heard her," he said. "She wants us all in the drawing room."

We all trooped into the exquisite drawing room where I had arrived for my interview. So much had happened since then. It felt almost as if that was a different person. I looked around the room remembering the wariness I had felt.

"Is something funny, Charlotte?" Jillian asked.

I turned to meet her gaze. "No, there isn't." I could feel the other staff exchanging peculiar looks with each other.

She went straight to the point. "My emerald bracelet is missing."

I didn't think it was possible for the room to become quieter, but it did. Everyone froze.

Jillian went on. "I was away for a little while so that's probably when—"

Mr. Boothsworth spoke up. "Madam, I'll review the security footage and handle this myself."

"No, Barnaby," she said coldly. "I'll handle this myself. I don't want to waste time and I won't house a thief a moment longer than necessary. I've sent some of the security guards from our London offices to all your rooms to investigate. We should be able to figure out the truth very soon."

All our mouths dropped open in shock. She had sent strangers into our rooms without telling us, without having us there to see what they were doing with our private stuff. I shouldn't have been surprised, but I was. I think I already knew what the outcome of this 'search' was going to be. Around me people shifted, but I did not move. I just stared at her. She wouldn't look me in the eye. She opened a book and started reading it.

Less than ten minutes later two of the security personnel she had talked about came into the drawing room with the missing bracelet in hand.

Of course. They found the bracelet in my room, tucked away in my suitcase. The rest of the staff was asked to leave. I boldly met her gaze.

For a while the only sound was the tapping of her feet against the floor. Then I spoke. I wasn't going to give her the satisfaction of lording it over me. "I didn't take your jewelry, but regardless, I'll quit. Thanks for the opportunity. I enjoyed working here in spite of everything."

"No," she refuted furiously. "You're not quitting. I'm firing you. The rest of the staff have witnessed this incident so humbly tuck your tail between your legs and get out of my home. I will extend some mercy to you. I'll keep this out of my assessment of your performance if you agree never to come back here, or try to contact my husband again, otherwise I'll make sure everyone knows you are a dangerous thief. Also you'll fuck their husbands behind their backs. I will ruin you, I swear it on my life."

I watched her, wondering how a woman could have been so blessed and yet so ungrateful? How could she not see how incredibly lucky she was? She was willing to throw it all away for cheap sex with men who probably didn't give a shit about her. I had already opened my mouth to tell her where she could stick her stupid threat, when Zackary ran into the room.

"Charlotte, are you coming with Mummy and me for the picnic?" he asked.

I shook my head. "No, darling. This time it is just going to be you and Mummy."

"Awww," he groaned with disappointment.

Mrs. King glared at her son. I knew that she was fuming uncontrollably underneath. "Zackary, don't be such a crybaby. Stand up straight. Look at your hands. They look filthy. Let me see them. Come here."

The boy went over to her, and she put him on her lap and started to clean his hands. For a few seconds I stared at them. Their blonde heads close together. Zackary was her son. Not mine. No matter how much I pretended to myself, he was not mine and she would never allow him to feel anything for me but hate. I had to end this here. It had already gone too far. I knew I couldn't stay under her roof for a moment longer.

"Take care of Zackary," I said to her. "He's a wonderful boy."

"Go," she ordered without looking up.

Outside the security personnel were waiting for me. They escorted me up to my room where my things were already packed. After confirming there was nothing left behind, the security personnel picked up my luggage and escorted me down the stairs. I met the rest of the staff at the foot of the stairs. I wished they had not bothered, because I was already so close to tears.

Mrs. Blackmore gave me a hug. "I know you had nothing to do with it," she said, and it consoled me when I saw the same vote of confidence reflected in the eyes of the other staff.

"Give me your address," Carrie said.

And I was about to, when Mrs. King's voice rang out. "Don't you dare communicate with the thief. Unless you want to join her."

Carrie went white. I just smiled at her and walked out of the house.

I wished so desperately to be able to see Brett. Even if it was for one last time. This wouldn't be happening if he was here. He'd know the last thing I would do is steal his wife's jewelry. Hell, if I wanted jewelry, all I had to do was ask April. She'd shower me with them.

I got into the dark car waiting for me. The driver said nothing. Then the massive gates were sliding shut behind me. Fighting back tears I turned around to gaze at the old dark castle. It had opened me to passions I'd never experienced before. My instinct had been right that day when I'd first arrived here and I'd had the impression if I entered these gates I'd leave a different person.

I was leaving as a different person.

I refused to allow the tears to fall because if I did, I didn't know how I was going to make them stop.

CHAPTER 48

BRETT

I immediately noticed the somber mood the moment I arrived back at the castle.

Barnaby greeted me as usual in front of my wing, but I could see instantly that he was distracted, his usually razor sharp gaze darting around. I had only been away two days because I cut my trip short, but it already felt like far too many days.

"Is everything alright?" I asked.

He swallowed hard. "I'm sorry to say, Sir, that Madam sent Miss Conrad packing yesterday ago for … stealing her jewelry."

What the fuck? I couldn't go away for two fucking days without Jillian fucking up my life and ruining even that little bit of happiness I had carved for myself. She was a selfish bitch. She didn't want me and didn't want anyone else to have me. Anger ripped through me.

"I'm very certain that Miss Conrad had absolutely nothing to do with the thef—" he was saying, but I was already striding towards Jillian's wing.

As I passed Zackary's wing, I could hear the sound of him crying. I changed direction and went to his room. The door was slightly ajar and I knocked softly before I went in. He was alone on his bed. When he saw me his crying subsided as though he was afraid of how I would react to his tears. I went forward and took a seat on his bed. He quickly scooted over, sniffing heavily as he gazed up at me.

"What's the matter?" I asked.

I could see exactly what the problem was in his eyes, but he appeared too afraid to speak.

I lifted my hand, and when he didn't withdraw, cautiously wiped the tears from his face. "You miss Charlotte, don't you?"

He bobbed his head in response as more tears leaked out of his eyes.

"Then why didn't you stop her from leaving? I left you in charge."

He gazed innocently up at me. "I didn't know she had gone." He dropped his voice to a whisper. "Mummy says she is a thief."

"She isn't," I said firmly. "It was all a misunderstanding. Mummy made a mistake."

He looked at me hopefully. "So can she come back?"

"I don't see why not," I said and smiled.

The door was suddenly pushed open then, and I turned to

see Jillian, her face scrubbed of makeup and her arms folded across her chest. She was ready for a fight. It was one where she needed to be stripped bare and the only one that she knew she had even the ghost of a chance in winning with me.

"You shouldn't have consoled him," she said. "I was going to let him tire himself out."

"Zackary, can you please go downstairs to Mrs. Blackmore," I instructed, "I need to speak to your mother."

Sniffing, he looked between me and his mother and climbed out of the bed. With his fire truck in hand, he made his way out of the room leaving Jillian and I alone.

"I thought I made myself clear when I told you I didn't want you here any longer," I began.

Folding her arms across her chest, she leaned against the door frame to watch me, and for an instant I saw once again the selfish but still endearing girl that I had grown up with. That I once convinced myself I loved in my own little way.

"I'm not divorcing you, Brett," she stated. "Maybe I would have a few days ago, but not anymore. Not now that I've realized whom you're replacing me with."

Her voice broke dramatically. She hugged herself as if she was cold. But I was not buying any of it. I knew her too long. It was all an act.

"How could you?" she accused. "I hired Charlotte, I brought her into this home, and then the both of you go behind my back and do this?"

"What exactly have we done, Jillian?" I asked wearily.

Fighting with her seemed so pointless. I just wanted to never see her again. "Please tell me."

"I saw the way you looked at her," she cried, tears rolling down her face. She swiped at them angrily. "I don't need to see any more to understand what is going on ... cause ... because you used to look at me that way. She's changed everything in the house. I was only gone for a few days and she turned it all upside down. This is my house and my family."

I didn't want to squabble with her but still it was the closure she needed and I would give it to her. "Upside down? *You* were the one who turned everything upside down."

She couldn't disagree with me, so instead she stared straight into my eyes as she allowed herself to tremble in an Oscar worthy performance. "I messed up," she admitted. "I took you ... all of this for granted ... but still it's mine, Brett. It's always been. Don't take it away."

"What is the name of Charlotte's agency?"

She looked at me as though she couldn't believe what I had just asked her. "You expect me to tell you? You can torture me and I'll never reveal it. You'll never find her," she swore. "I'll make sure of it."

With a sigh, I started to walk out of the room but she grabbed me. I could smell the alcohol on her breath then. It was all so pointless.

"Let me go, Jillian," I said between clenched teeth.

"She doesn't truly care about you. How could you be so blind? Don't you know what you look like?"

I jerked my hand away.

She realized she had said the wrong thing. "You're a billion-aire, Brett. What woman in the world wouldn't want you? That was why even I gave my heart to you in the first place, but then I changed. I saw you as a beautiful person. Let's start over ..." she pleaded.

She grabbed my hand again. This time I yanked it away so hard, the force of my annoyance sent her to the ground.

Looking down at her groveling on the floor, I gave out my last warning. "I don't want to see you here when I get back, otherwise there will be no money for you, Jillian. Nothing."

"I'll take Zackary with me," she screamed.

"Before you do that you should get your lawyer to explain to you what our pre-nup entitles you to, and what you could reasonably expect to leech off me. I think you will find out very quickly that I apparently own no assets at all, but play nice and I'll make sure you're very well taken care of for the rest of your life. You'll have full visiting rights, which considering how much time you actually spend with Zackary, should be perfectly adequate for your needs."

She was sobbing and shouting obscenities when I walked out of there.

CHAPTER 49

JILLIAN

https://www.youtube.com/watch?v=MEMUsC8ppU0
Don't Cry For Me Argentina

I was on the ground groveling, crying, and screaming for him … and he just walked out.

It was just too unbelievable. Could it really be that he didn't care anymore? I stopped crying and stood up. I think I was in a state of shock. He'd been locked away in his wing, almost a cripple for so long, I never even imagined the day would come when he'd be strong enough to move forward without me.

I was Zackary's mother.

He needed me. Even if he didn't love me, he loved Zackary with all his heart.

I could always get him back through Zackary. It was that bitch! She gave him strength. Until she came he was weak and dependent on me. He still needed me. But she had come and given him ideas. Made him think he deserved more. She laid with him and made him believe he was not a monster.

I had to find a way to make it right again.

I thought about threatening to reveal to Zackary he was not his father, but that would be self-defeating. Zackary might want to know who his father was and I didn't know either. Also, I was smart enough to realize that Zackary was my real power over him and I had no intention of giving that up.

I walked to the drawer and pulled out a bottle of gin. I unscrewed the top and drank straight from the bottle.

"Mummy?"

I swallowed. "Yes, darling."

"Is Daddy mad with you?

I put the bottle on the table. "I'm afraid he is mad with both of us."

"Why?"

"I think someone's been saying really bad things about us."

His eyes grew round. "Who?"

"I don't know, you know that Charlotte stole Mummy's bracelet, right?'

He swallowed hard and refused to look at me. I stared at him in shock. My God, that bitch had turned my own son against me. "Zackary look at me."

He lifted his head up. "You do know that Charlotte stole Mummy's bracelet, right?" I repeated.

"Daddy said it was a misunderstanding."

For a moment I couldn't believe my own ears. Terrible rage hit the base of my brain. My hand closed over the gin bottle and I threw it across the room. Zackary screamed and ran out of the room. Barnaby arrived at the door.

"Is everything okay, Madam?" he asked.

I knew he was a traitor too. I'd seen him hugging and kissing that bitch when she was leaving. "Get out, you worthless servant," I screamed.

Expressionlessly, he nodded his stupid head and backed away. It made me even more angry. I needed more than a drink. I wanted to be back in London. I wanted Anton to tie me to his cross and punish me until I screamed and climaxed because the pain was too much. I found my cellphone and booked Anton for that evening. Then I went to the bar and I began to drink. I drank a whole bottle of Brett's best Scotch. It tasted like shit, but I wanted to feel happy again.

I had never been happy in my life. Little insignificant creatures like the nanny could find happiness, but never me. I started to sob. I could feel the pain coming from deep inside. I hated that bitch. I knew where she lived. I wanted to go and teach her a lesson.

How dare she?

I gave her a job and she stole my man and my son. Ungrateful thief. I just couldn't understand it. How could Brett even look at her with her fat legs, her coarse features, and her cheap clothes? I stood up and the room tilted. I knew her address. I would go to her and kick her simpering face in.

I took one step, then another.

Mr. Boothsworth caught up with me at the front door. "Where are you going, Madam?"

Irritating idiot. "Bring my car around."

He frowned. "I don't think you should."

I grabbed him by his tie. "Listen you little rat. Bring my car around or you're fired."

A very strange expression crossed his eyes.

I blinked in shock and let go of his clothing. I staggered back and stared at him. I must have been very drunk, because the look he gave me was one of loathing. As if I was a piece of gum stuck to his good shoe.

"I'll bring the car around Madam," he said softly, then he was gone.

I waited alone for someone to bring my car around. I wished Brett was home. I wished I had been a good wife to him. I wished I had never hired the nanny. I wished I could love Zackary the way other mothers loved their children. I wished I wasn't so fucked up.

A strong wind blew at my face. It made my hair fly into my face. I turned towards the wind, and it flattened my clothes against my body. For an instant I felt more alive than I had ever been. I turned my face up to the heavens. Then my red Mercedes sports came to a stop in front of me. One of the staff, Brian or whatever his name was, got out and I fell into the driver's seat.

I closed the door and stepped on the gas. Life was good. Everything was going to be fine for me. Tomorrow I would find a way to win Brett back.

CHAPTER 50

CHARLOTTE

https://www.youtube.com/watch?v=fDxzQJaA228
I knew you were waiting for me

When I got back to my apartment all I did was sleep for nearly three days, because I was unable to do anything else.

April's eyes widened in surprise when I opened the front door, headache throbbing and eyes swollen from too much sleeping and crying.

"Why are you here so early?" I asked.

"Because no matter when I call I get your answering machine," she said shutting the door and following me into the living room. With a sigh, I continued on to retrieve the leftover pizza from the previous night, and put it into the microwave.

"Are you ready to talk yet?" she asked me and I shook my head. "There's nothing to talk about."

"That hurts."

I turned to her. "Oh babe, it's not because I don't want to share it with you, you know that. I just want to forget about it all for now. Once it's all sorted out in my brain and I get back to normal I'll tell you everything."

"I'm here for you, okay," she said and came over to force me into a hug. Her big stomach kept the hug oddly A shaped. I tried and failed to get away so I just relaxed into her arms, the familiar embrace reminding me of the one I had received from my mother yesterday.

"Are you sure there is nothing I can do?" she pushed.

"Yup."

"Can I just ask one tiny, little question?"

I glared at her. "One. Just one. Don't ask any more questions after it."

She pulled away and lifted her hand. "I swear, I won't."

"What is it?"

"Did you fall in love with him?"

I ran my hands through my untidy hair. "Yes. I fell in love with him, but we're from two different worlds. Don't worry, I don't regret it or anything, I just truly hope that he'll be alright."

She was quiet as I turned back to the microwave and just as I had expected she couldn't hold back.

"But he didn't break up with you ... his wife was the one who—"

"Please, April. You're not making it any better. Just leave it, okay. It was a very complicated situation and maybe this is for the best, for everyone concerned."

She bit her tongue while I plated my pizza.

"I just have one more question," she said finally.

I frowned at her. Now she was just taking the piss.

"I'm so sorry but this is really the last one. Speaking from experience, powerful men don't let go of what they want. If he finds you and wants you back, what will you do?"

My heart jumped into my throat. I opened my mouth, but no words would come out.

I stood there gaping like a demented goldfish until she came to me and put her arms around me. "I'm sorry, Charlotte. I should have kept my big mouth shut."

"It's okay. It's okay. I'll be fine. Time will sort me out." I flashed her a fake smile. We went into the living room and I chewed uninterestedly at my pizza while I listened to her talk about Yuri and her baby. I was glad she had come. It took my mind off Brett. I had pushed the plate away when the doorbell rang.

I groaned. "It's that damn new postman again. Why can't he just leave it behind the flowerpot like the other one used to do?"

"I'll go," she called as she headed off to answer the door.

I picked up my empty plate to go to the kitchen, when April

called out to me. Something in her voice made me stop in my tracks. Slowly, I moved towards the hallway. One step at a time. It was not the new postman.

Standing at my apartment door was the man I had not been able to keep out of my mind for more than three seconds for the last three days.

She couldn't stop looking at him as she spoke, while his gaze had already moved past her to me.

"You have a guest," she said.

I gripped the plate hard. I couldn't breathe.

"Charlotte?"

"Yeah, I'm here," I squeaked out.

"Okay, I'll leave now," she said, giving me a wink. "I don't think I can stand here and watch you turn into a creepy awestruck stranger."

She went through the door and he came in. I tried to settle my erratically beating heart, but it was beating so hard I wouldn't have been surprised if he could hear it. I took a deep breath as my eyes hungrily roved over him. He was dressed immaculately in a double-breasted navy blue suit. His presence seemed to dwarf my entire apartment. My hands itched, the need to touch him an almost possessing force.

"Brett," I said.

"You left," he accused.

"I wasn't exactly given a choice. How did you find me?"

He shrugged. "I found the name of the agency from a letterhead Jillian had left in the drawing room, but the agency wouldn't give me your address so I bought it."

I shook my head at the lives of rich people. "Just like that, huh?"

"What did you expect me to do? Just leave it?"

"No, but…"

"You made no attempt to contact me," he said. Something dark slipped into his eyes then and it made me sad. I truly, truly more than anything else … more than even my desire to be with him, wanted him to be happy. Thoroughly and boundlessly.

"You were not really mine and I was put in my place."

He took a step towards me. "You're mine," he said harshly. "If you didn't want to be then you shouldn't have worked your way into my heart in the first place. But as you did, I'm not letting you go."

Hot tears filled my eyes. My heart felt like it was ready to burst. "I don't know that she will let us be. She will always be in the way poisoning you and Zackary."

"I apologize that you had to deal with Jillian. It must have been so humiliating for you, but Jillian will never trouble us again."

"How can you say that? She is Zackary's mother. She will always be in the picture."

"After I found out you'd gone, I told her to move out. She got very drunk and stormed out of the castle and ordered Barnaby to bring her car to her. Unfortunately for her, she met with a really bad accident. She got thrown out of her car just like I had. But unlike me she damaged her spinal cord."

"What?" I gasped, my hand coming over my mouth.

"Yeah, it's hard to even imagine it, but Jillian is paralyzed from the neck down."

"Oh, my God!"

"It was her own fault. She liked riding the danger train in more ways than one and it was only a matter of time before something bad happened to her."

"Where is she now?"

"In one of the best hospitals money can buy."

"That's horrible. I detested her, but I didn't want that for her."

"When I went to see her she thought I had come to gloat, but I took no pleasure in seeing her like that. When I was in a wheelchair she showed no pity or empathy so it was as if fate decided to teach her what it feels like to be helpless and stuck inside a body that doesn't work. I will pay to keep her in the best care possible. I owe that to her father."

"What about Zackary?"

"He's confused and frightened, but time will take care of that."

"Poor thing," I whispered.

"So you see. I am the only one you need to worry about now. It's me and you … and nothing else, and no one else. Do you understand?"

I couldn't help smiling. "Who lives that way?"

"We will," he said. "You and me and Zackary and all the other children we will have together."

He came forward and pulled me into his arms, lightly moving his nose from my hair and down my face to my neck, inhaling, and reveling."

"How I missed you," he said. "I would have come to you sooner but all these other events were in the way."

I pulled away to stare into his eyes. "You've known her since you both were children. She has to be more than an unfortunate event to you."

"She is," he responded, and I could see the deep sadness in his gaze that he was as usual trying to hold at bay … to mask. "Especially when I think of her father. She will have the best care and assistance that she needs, but my road together with her ended a long time ago, even before ours began."

I released a deep breath which made my entire frame quiver.

That made him laugh. "Relax," he said to me and placed the lightest of kisses on my forehead that made me want more.

"I love you, Charlotte Conrad."

"Me too. I love you so much I could die."

"Don't you dare do that."

I grinned.

"We'll take it one day at a time, okay," he stated.

"I couldn't ask for more," I replied, and slid my arms around his neck.

"You've been crying," he noted as his gaze searched mine.

I nodded, comforted by his warmth and strength. The tears and sadness seemed far away.

"Never again," he ordered.

Nodding obediently, I crushed my lips to his and gave in to the incomparable taste of home.

EPILOGUE

BRETT

I Say a Little Prayer For You
https://www.youtube.com/watch?v=KtBbyglq37E

4 years later

I
t was our second day in Languedoc, and our first return to the South of France since our wedding three years earlier. The villa was one of our favorite homes.

A short distance from us, our Chef was working the grill and the smells of meat cooking filled my nostrils. With my eyes shut and a pair of sunglasses shielding them from the late afternoon sun I lounged in the warm infinity pool overlooking the deep blue of the Mediterranean.

My kids, there were three of them, looked very small playing together on the beach beyond. They were watched by Mr. and Mrs. Boothsworth. Yup, they made it official and tied the knot.

Sliding the sunglasses up to my head, I looked down at the woman clinging to me. Her beautiful gold hair was damp and clinging to her neck from an earlier swim. My arms were spread out as I leaned against the edge of the pool, while her arms were around my neck and head rested on my shoulder.

Every inch of her was plastered to me, my cock resting against her stomach, was slowly getting harder and harder. She felt my gaze, and lifted her head to meet my eyes, a dazzling smile across her lips. This woman had plucked me from the dark, lonely hell that was my life and put me into a brand new world full of light and color. She single-handedly changed my life.

Loving all of me, even my scars. She even managed to change Zackary's fear of me. One day, when he was six, he asked me to show him my scars. I took off my mask and he looked at me for a long time, then he smiled and said, "Charlotte was totally right. They are like one of the paintings hanging in the modern art gallery she took me to." I laughed then. Only Charlotte could ever come up with the idea that my ugly face was a work of art.

"Sleepy?" I asked her.

She nodded lazily.

I brushed her hair behind her ears. "We just got up from a long siesta. Why are you already exhausted?"

She looked at me from underneath her lashes. It could have been the sun in her eyes, but I was going to take that as an invitation, and I never passed up invitations from my wife.

Holding her neck in place, my tongue slipped into her mouth and danced with hers, teasing, tasting, and loving. Putting both my hands into the water, I grabbed her cushiony ass to crush her hips to mine.

She ground herself against me. Rock hard, I let lust guide me as usual to the threshold of pleasure. She was my drug.

When I came up for air my mind was made up, I was going to take her right here in the water. I shifted position, her back replacing mine against the wall of the pool. Shielding her from view, I turned towards the cook.

"Édouard," I called.

He turned to look and I gave him a wave with my hand. He got the message and nodded.

Grabbing her thighs, I pulled her feet off the floor and wound them around my hips. A beautiful moan sounded in her throat as my swollen cock settled in the crook of her delicious cunt.

She bounced her hips, her head thrown back in brazen delight. I loved seeing her this way, completely woman. She kissed me fervently, showing her love for me once more in a way that words could not express. As always it humbled me.

I pulled my cock out of my trunks underneath the water, and slid her bikini bottom aside to allow it access to its home, but, she *blocked* it! Halfway out of my mind I searched her gaze for a reason. The furrows in my forehead were her warning that it had better be a good one.

"I have something to tell you," she said.

"You can try to speak when I'm fucking you, otherwise it has to wait," I growled. I tried to push against her once more, but she stopped me with surprising determination. Holding me at bay she sought to lock my gaze with hers.

"Baby," I complained.

She cracked up in laughter.

Finding nothing at all amusing I watched her impatiently.

"I'm laughing at the term of endearment," she said.

"What?" I asked.

"Because I'm not sure which of us exactly you're referring to …"

I backed away from her then. When women resorted to speaking in riddles. "This better be worth the interruption otherwise you're not going to be able to walk for the rest of this trip."

"How will you explain my temporary inability to walk to the kids?" she asked.

I looked ahead at the twin girls and baby boy assisting Zackary at the castle he was making.

"I don't owe them one."

She leaned forward and whispered into my ear. "What about the one currently with us?"

My heart stuttered to a stop. "What are you saying?"

Her gaze on me was searing, threatening to fry my brain to fucking ashes.

"You're fucking pregnant?"

She couldn't hold back her smile. Pure unadulterated joy ripped through me.

"Really?" I shouted in disbelief.

She nodded, her eyes gleaming. "Yes, I'm fucking pregnant. Although, I have no idea how it happened. We only fuck like seven times a week."

Tears rushed to my eyes, I lowered my head and rested my forehead against hers.

"Hey," she said softly, her voice softening at my unexpected reaction.

She cradled me like one of our children. "Just to be sure, are these happy or sad tears? Because I know you're already struggling to find enough sleep with the colony we're raising."

My response was soul deep. "I never expected in my life that I would know what it feels like to be this happy."

She leaned away to stare into my eyes. "Oh, Brett. I am the luckiest girl in the whole universe."

"Thank you," I said, the tears falling silently past my scars. She put her hand out to wipe them away, the warmth of her touch on my face that had once chased away the cold felt like silk. "I love you with all of my heart."

At that moment tears filled her eyes too. Then she said back the words that I would never get tired of hearing, or take for granted. "I love you even more."

The End

COMING SOON...

So ... my next book is titled:

A Kiss Stolen
December, 2018

****

Remember Liliana Eden
When she was eleven years old.

I look at the grubby boy. He is tall and broad with fierce black eyes and straight black hair. He must be at least a couple of years older than me. I think he's the son of one of the traveling gypsies. His father did some work for my father. He is standing in the garden. His clothes are dirty and his hands are grubby, but for some strange reason I don't understand why I feel drawn to him. I decide to walk up to him and offer him some food.

"What's your name?" I ask.

"None of your business," he says rudely.

"What a rude little boy you are," I say scornfully. "I only came over to see if you are hungry."

"I'm not hungry. I don't need your charity."

I put my hands on my hips feeling angry at his rudeness. "I was only trying to be nice."

His eyes flash. "You want to be nice?"

I look at him, confused. "Well, I did. I'm not sure I want to anymore."

"Then piss off."

I gasp. I don't know why I didn't just walk away and tell Daddy. "Why are you being so rude?"

"Why are you being such a pest?"

"All right I want to be nice. What do you want?"

Suddenly he grabs me and kisses me on the mouth! I am too surprised to resist. His mouth is firm and forceful and hot. Something flutters in my belly. Then he lifts his head and looks into my eyes. I can't look away. I'm too astonished.

"Liliana Eden, I'm going to marry you one day," he declares, before striding away.

I touch my lips. They are still tingling. He kissed me. Ewww … Yuck. The rude boy kissed me! I run towards our house as fast as I can. I fly in through the door and burst into the kitchen. Both Mommy and Daddy are there. "A boy kissed me," I announce breathlessly.

"What?" Daddy shouts and jumps up, his face dark with fury.

Mommy grabs hold of his wrist. "She's only eleven, Jake. It doesn't mean anything."

"Fuck it doesn't." Daddy swears furiously as strides out of the house.

I watch him march up to the boy's father. They talk, Daddy gesturing angrily. The man calls his son and slaps him upside the head. The boy says nothing. He just turns his head and looks at me through the window. There is no smile on his face. He just stares at me until his father slaps him again and pulls him away.

I touch my lips. They are still tingling. I wish I had not told Daddy about him.

And the Eden saga continues with the:

A Kiss Stolen

For those of you who are familiar with the Crystal Jake (Eden) Series you will know Liliana as Jake's daughter. This is Liliana's story.
Note: it can be read as a standalone, but your enjoyment will be enhanced by reading the Crystal Jake series.

Get The Series at Amazon:

Crystal Jake

****

If you want to read about when April met her Russian billionaire, you can find it here:

Nanny & The Beast

And if you have already read the Crystal Jake Series and
Nanny & The Beast,
then have you met Blake Law Barrington,

The Billionaire Banker

60601668R00173